GERMAN FANTASIA

Also by Philippe Claudel in English translation

Grey Souls
Brodeck's Report
Monsieur Linh and His Child
The Investigation
Parfums
The Tree of the Toraja
Dog Island

Philippe Claudel

GERMAN FANTASIA

Translated from the French by
Julian Evans

MACLEHOSE PRESS
QUERCUS · LONDON

First published in the French language as *Fantaisie Allemande*
by Éditions Stock, 2020
First published in Great Britain in 2023 by

MacLehose Press
An imprint of Quercus Publishing Ltd
Carmelite House
50 Victoria Embankment
London EC4Y 0DZ

An Hachette UK company

A CIP catalogue record for this book is available from the British Library.

ISBN (MMP) 978 1 52941 788 3
ISBN (Ebook) 978 1 52941 789 0

Designed and typeset in Quadraat by Libanus Press Ltd
Printed and bound in Great Britain by Clays Ltd, Elcograf S.p.A.

MIX
Paper from
responsible sources
FSC® C104740

Papers used by MacLehose Press are from well-managed forests
and other responsible sources.

To Luigi Spagnol (1961–2020),
friend and Italian publisher

Germany has a whiff of the abyss.

THOMAS BERNHARD

There is, beyond the Rhine,
an atmosphere of drama and melancholy.
All the ordinary things of life there
take on the colours of the setting sun.
Depending on his or her mood, the traveller
may find this charming
or alarming.

PIERRE MAC ORLAN

CONTENTS

EIN MANN

IT WASN'T THE COLD THAT HAD WOKEN HIM BUT a confused feeling that wouldn't go away, though his sleepiness was gradually wearing off. The coat had grown heavier and was weighing on his clothes underneath, and on his chest too, like a leaden straitjacket. It took him a while to work out that the heaviness was coming from the coarse wool cloth that had gradually got waterlogged, so the coat had doubled in weight, making him feel imprisoned, as if he had drowned in it. Then, groping his way, he surfaced from the dream he had surrendered to, a sensation of faint warmth really, more than an actual dream. He started to shiver. He was soaked. His eyes opened onto blackness. His heart pounded. His wound had opened too and was stinging and weeping again.

It was two days and two nights now he had been under the fir tree. It was an old tree whose lower branches were stuck to the ground, entangled with roots whose shapes reminded him of varicose veins. He had had to drag some of them aside so he could snuggle into the space next to the gnarled trunk. Here the ground formed a large hollow covered with dry needles that made a soft mattress, on which he had stretched out full length. The needles were warm. They gave off a smell of resin and bark. Of autumn too. A scent that gradually faded.

He had told himself that as long as he stayed there, nothing bad could happen to him. The thought had made him forget his hunger. He had three potatoes left in one of his pockets. He'd found them a few days earlier, digging in a field with his fingers, on all fours, like an animal, and had decided to keep them until he needed them.

Under the fir tree, for the first time in a long time he had stopped being on his guard. As soon as he had managed to wriggle in under the branches of the tree, he had realised that it was impossible for anyone to guess he was there. Even someone walking past a couple of metres away wouldn't notice him. He had fallen into a deep sleep.

The forest quivered in the rain. The fir tree's branches had stopped the droplets for a while, but eventually they had dripped their way past them and trickled down to where he was, soaking through the coat, the two sweaters underneath, the shirt and into his underpants and under-shirt. He turned up the coat's collar as high as it would go, but all it did was make him wetter, tipping rivulets of water down the back of his neck.

He pulled his knees up to his stomach and kept his eyes open. Everything around him was black. The rain and the night had made the forest around him disappear, and the November cold that blew around his face felt colder now. The bed of needles had turned muddy. Around him it smelled like a pit. He shivered until the first glimmers of dawn, and when daybreak finally came, it was a feeble, miserable day.

He crawled out of his hiding place. He stood up with difficulty and took some faltering steps. It was as if he had to learn how to walk all over again. A milky light gradually outlined the trees against the darkness. The mist created the intermittent illusion that they were advancing on him, like huge statues rolling forwards on their plinths. In the sky, crows scraped the bellies of the clouds. He tried to twist the flaps of the coat to wring them out, but his fingers were too numb and had no strength in them. He walked away from the fir tree, the way you walk away from a friend who no longer cares and who can do no more for you. The rain had stopped. His teeth chattered.

He forced himself to walk quickly, hoping it would help him warm up. The coat flapped against his legs, and water worked its way into his boots, which he had not taken off for days for fear that they might be stolen. Yet he had met no-one during his escape. All he had glimpsed, a week earlier as he rested behind a rock, was a column of vehicles several hundred metres away, rolling through a dip in the landscape overgrown with bracken. He couldn't have said which army they were from: Russians probably. They left, and the silence returned. The wind had eventually blown away the petrol smell that drifted up to him.

Most of the time he had slept in woods, ditches, abandoned barns, in the lee of a low wall. On the outskirts of places that had once been towns and were now unrecognisable. From a distance, the apartment blocks looked like decayed teeth. From their carious depths, lift cages rose into nothingness. Everything was smoking.

The countryside, which was also deserted, was a less awful sight. He couldn't have said why. All the villages he had passed through were just as ruined, and every trace of human life had retreated from them. The roads that led to them had been shelled, methodically pulverised, reduced to strange rivers in the grip of a new kind of debacle, the ice floes replaced by thousands of broken lumps of tarmac. Here and there among them were strewn the mutilated carcasses of buses, trucks, military vehicles or cars, still full of their occupants, reduced to swollen and unrecognisable corpses.

In one of these villages he had found the coat. He had gone into a house that a bomb had sliced in two as if it had been sitting on a butcher's block. He had rummaged through the cupboards and drawers of every overturned piece of furniture. There was nothing left. He had come in the wake of numerous other strays, soldiers, vagrants, deserters. But underneath a filthy mattress he had turned over without much hope was the coat. The sleeves were folded up, as if it had just been taken out of its box. A black coat, too big for him, in an old-fashioned style. He had put it on straight away, discarding there and then his padded soldier's jacket, from which he had torn off the stripes and badges long before. Just as he had destroyed his identity papers, service record, identity tag engraved with his service number, every object that could have identified his former life. He had even used a knife to cut out the tattoo of his blood group that he carried on the inside of his arm, near his armpit. This was the wound that didn't want to heal. It was a constant reminder of his recent past.

Walking hour after hour, day after day, let him forget time and hunger. He was no longer anything more than two legs walking over the earth, a body in motion, topped by a burning, grimy head in which the same anxious thoughts went round and round as if in a cage.

He walked on through the forest, trying to stay in a straight line, more to give himself the illusion that he wasn't getting lost than to follow a real direction. He told himself that by doing this he would have to emerge eventually from these endless woods. He came across no paths, apart from the tracks of game. Pine forest gave way to beech forest. Then it was thickets overrun by brambles, then pines again, gloomy and planted in tight rows.

The day stayed drab and low, and in the sky there were always crows, which he glimpsed in black flocks, swirling like clouds of ashes. As he walked, he tried to estimate the hours, and from that to work out the kilometres. He had to be a long way now from the place he had run from. Probably three or four weeks' walking through this region of hills and valleys and woods.

When he guessed it was gone midday, he stopped in a clearing. Between some mosses he found a spring. He drank for a long time. Then he looked at himself in the water's mirror. He saw a thin face. Hair that had grown every which way. Ill-defined features, ageless. A mouth from which mist drifted. Nothing else. He sat on a stone and ate half a potato.

The raw flesh tasted of flour, sweet and grainy. He chewed it to a mush which he kept in his mouth for a long time. He had never eaten anything so wretched and he had never enjoyed eating anything so much. A suffering and a pleasure that he made last as long as he could, that filled his thoughts and made him forget the state he was in. He stayed sitting on the stone, beside the spring murmuring its heedless melody, with the taste of potato mush in his mouth.

Then the memory came back to him of the prisoners who were capable of killing each other when you threw leftovers from a meal or the peelings from the camp kitchens in among them. This always amused Viktor. He would arrive with the bowl, call them the way you would call hens or pigs, and tip its contents over the wire fence. The scrum would be incredible, silent but more vicious than dogs fighting. One or two were always left lying on the square. Sometimes Viktor would vary the entertainment by calling them, waiting till they were pressed against the wire, then dropping the contents at his feet so they could see it but it was beyond their reach as their hands pummelled the fence. This made Viktor laugh even more. He would watch the spectacle. He would laugh a little, to make Viktor happy.

He shivered. Cleared his throat, spat. He stood up abruptly and started walking again. His clothes hadn't dried. He had got used to their wet heaviness.

After perhaps an hour he thought he could see something white in the distance, and he slowed down. At first he felt it was a mirage produced by his tiredness. He went on towards the whiteness, leaning on the stick he had picked up a little while before, which gave him the look of a shepherd without a flock. In places the ground, covered with mouldy leaves, gave way under his feet.

All that whiteness beyond the forest's edge was a wide plain onto which the first snow was falling and which, in the gathering twilight, looked phosphorescent as it fell. He stopped near the last trees, still under their shelter. He hesitated to leave the forest he had spent so long walking through, and which had hidden him so completely from view.

Ahead of him, the horizon at the end of the snow-dusted fields merged with the sky, which had the same indistinct, slack texture. Their long, open, flat colour seemed to symbolise the anxiety of a boundless land, its framework dismembered. He turned back to the forest one last time. He caught himself feeling a tinge of sadness and sorrow, but set out across the fields nevertheless.

Very quickly, after only a few steps, he was walking more heavily. Earth so brown it was almost black clung to his boots. The field had not been ploughed for a long time. It had relaxed, reverted and become lumpy. The dusting of snow made a melting skin that soaked into the clods of clay or turned into dirty runnels and flowed into puddles that looked like miniature ponds.

Each step cost him effort. His stick was no help. He sometimes had the impression that the field wanted to swallow him up, that the earth, which probably had not been cultivated since the outbreak of hostilities, just wanted one thing, to gobble his body up, suck out all its juices, gulp it down and feast on it, to make the men he represented pay for the neglect in which they had left it.

He looked as far ahead as he could but was unable to make out any path. He missed the forest, which at least gave him the illusion of making progress, with each tree that appeared and disappeared giving a rhythm to his journey. He could not see a single farm. Or road. No river either. No canals. Great unclaimed fields extended from one end of the horizon to the other.

An aching tiredness gripped him. He couldn't go on. His wound gnawed at him. His lungs hurt. Each breath compelled him to go deeper into them to fetch the scrap of air hidden there. He concentrated on the best path to take, metre by metre, in the cloying expanse. And once again he was filled with the feeling of blankness that had not left him since everything had collapsed.

He had spent the last years not asking himself any questions. Thanks to the coming of the new order, he had gained a status and respect that had previously been denied him. In next to no time he had been brought out of his near-invisibility, out of the mass of other men. He had been assigned a role and rank. He had been mass-produced, turned into an effective tool. He had been given orders. He carried them out. He hadn't felt the chaos coming. The great machine had crumbled.

Was he guilty? Guilty of having obeyed? Or guilty of not having disobeyed? All he had done was follow. Did that make him less responsible than the others? Less than Viktor? In the camp he had spent his time writing. Lists. He had to check names. Count men and women, children, old people. Sometimes he had to undertake interrogations. Try to find out if they were lying or telling the truth. Transcribe the interrogations. Open files. Assemble them. Divide them up. Establish groups, sub-groups. Convoys. Get the convoys ready for departure. Sometimes follow the convoys to where they were to be taken. Take by the hand, as they got down from the truck, the old people who had difficulty walking, the children too, because his mild face and calm voice reassured them, as did his gestures, which were never violent.

Then it was Viktor and his colleagues who took charge of everything. He stayed in the background. He saw nothing. He retraced his steps back to the truck well before Viktor began his work. He would smoke a cigarette, sometimes two. Doze. He heard the detonations muffled by the curtain of trees and mounds of gravel. Actually, he didn't always hear them. It depended where the wind was coming from, and whether he was even paying attention, so much did the rustling of the poplars' leaves carry him away from the place where he was.

It was painful to think about it all again, to consider that perhaps all that had just been a misunderstanding, that little by little, as a result of not knowing how to say no, he had reached a point where he could no longer tell the difference between what was done and what was not done, what was good and what was evil.

He could not feel the cold or mud anymore. He pushed on in his stupor. He felt a bit as if he was waking up after having been blind drunk for a decade. He wiped his hand across his forehead, to erase the images in his head and wipe away all these thoughts that were too big for his brain.

As night began to fall he kept pushing on in the middle of nowhere. A narrow strip of light spread across the horizon to the west. The wind had gone. Great low clouds, motionless now, scattered thin snowflakes that shrank from settling on the ground and melted on his forehead and his lips. He put his tongue out to catch the flakes, which became small, cool, watery pearls. He thought of the tears he had seen on many faces. Of the cries that had accompanied them.

In less than half an hour it would be impossible to see anything. Where would he sleep? It would be better for him to carry on walking, even if it meant falling asleep standing up. He had been walking like this for a while, between wakefulness and sleep, surprised to realise that the body could turn into a sort of automaton. At least if he went on walking he would not die of cold, unlike the men in rags who would halt and collapse all along the column after they had been ordered to evacuate the camp in the face of the enemy advance. You didn't even bother to prod them to their feet because you knew the winter would soon get the better of them. Sometimes, to relieve his boredom, Viktor would put a bullet in the back of one of their heads. And you carried on. Without having much idea where to.

Suddenly, as he made an effort to search the horizon one last time before darkness wiped out the world, he thought he could see, a few hundred metres away, a big square shape rising out of the last of the pale light. He regained some scraps of energy.

As he pressed on, the shape became more distinct, massive, windowless, and with a flat roof. It wasn't a farmhouse, more like a water tower, a silo or something like it.

By the time he finally got close to it, the night and the heavy earth had merged into one. He couldn't see further than five metres. The building loomed, imposing, in front of him. A sort of purring came from it, with crackling sounds from time to time, and sparks. A generator, or an electric transformer, protected by a double row of barbed wire that had been flattened in one place by a vehicle. He crept through the opening, moving with caution, his hands stretched in front of him because he could no longer make anything out.

When his fingers touched the wall at last, he felt a savage joy. The wall was warm, as if some wonderful fire was burning behind it. He pressed his two hands against it and moved along it sideways to find a door. He had forgotten his hunger, his exhaustion, his fear and suffering. It was almost as if he had returned after a long voyage to the threshold of the house where he had been born.

He was going to go inside. He had found a shelter. Heat. Peace. Protection. He imagined his mother's face, his father's too, his childhood, the evening meal, the hot soup and the glowing stove.

Suddenly the wall gave way to emptiness, from which a warm draught of air was blowing gently. The purring got louder. His hands groped in the dark and found what had to be a thick metal door, very slightly ajar. He tried pushing it several times with his shoulder but it refused to give, and the wound in his arm hurt him. The joy he felt gave way to panic. To be so close to comfort and reassurance, and not to be able to grasp it. He thought again of the prisoners staring at the peelings Viktor had tipped at his feet, of Viktor walking away from them and laughing, of their hands trying to pass through the wire.

He knelt and groped for a stone on the ground, some-thing that would allow him to force the door open. He was panting, cutting his hands on broken glass, grabbing hold of objects he could not identify exactly and then, suddenly, something like a rod, a tube made of metal, heavy and perhaps about two metres long. He could have wept for joy. He seized it, felt his way back to the opening, slid the iron tube into it and, with all the strength he was capable of, exerted an extraordinary force. The miracle happened. With a long grinding noise the door creaked open much wider than it had before, enough for him to push his way into the building.

He entered. The blackness became a velvet cloth that enveloped him. Nothing like the cold and soaking blackness of outside. Here it was another world. The heat was intense. Dry Delicious. The transformer's purring filled the air with a reassuring, animal music. He couldn't see anything, but he felt so good. For many long weeks he had not known such wellbeing.

He still held the iron rod in his hand. It was thanks to the rod that he had managed to get in. The object was suddenly endowed with magic powers. It would never have occurred to him to throw it away. It was simultaneously his divining rod, his sword, his sceptre, his blind man's cane with which he moved carefully forwards, using it to feel his way in the spongy blackness, step by step.

But suddenly the emptiness turned into a hard surface, and in a thousandth of a second the obscurity in which he had been picking his way ahead lit up as if by the light of a tremendous firework that flooded the space with an unbearable whiteness.

It happened so fast that the man had neither the time to understand what had happened to him nor the time to suffer: the massive electric current travelled right through his body and carbonised him instantly, transforming him into a charred shape welded to the iron rod and to the generator it had touched.

For several minutes afterwards, intermittent, fabulous showers of sparks burst and fell on what had been his body.

A sort of grand finale, without spectators.

Then the night returned, mellow and calm, and after a few last electrical sputterings, the purring sound of a big animal resumed, as if some mysterious digestive process had finally started.

SEX UND LINDEN

I'M NEARLY NINETY YEARS OLD. IT'S THE END OF May. I've always loved the month of May. I know I shan't get to see many more. Perhaps this is the last one. I'm not sad about it. I'm tired. To take a few steps these days, I need Anne to give me her arm. Or my son, when he drops by to see me. I hang on to her, or him, with my skinny hands. My fingers look like arthritic talons. I shake, and I open my mouth wide to breathe. I'm an exhausted fish, tossed down on the bank by a bad-tempered fisherman. My body wheezes and cracks. It takes a painfully long time to cover a few metres.

Anne is patient. It's what she does. She visits me three times a day. In the morning to wash me and give me breakfast. In the early afternoon to see that everything's okay and settle me for my nap. Later on, to come and keep me company for a while, do the washing-up and get me ready for bed. My son's not as gentle as she is. He's always in a hurry. His work takes up all his time. But he's my son. I'm happy to see him. I see that my slowness exasperates him – the way it's hard for me to find words, the way I shake and look at him without focusing properly. I think I scare him. He looks at me the way you look at a dead body and say to yourself, one of these days it's going to be me instead. It would scare anyone.

Anne's settled me in the garden on the lounger, near the bank of hydrangeas. I feel slightly too warm. Anne's always worried I'll catch cold. She's pulled the rug up to my chin. It's too much of an effort to extract one of my arms, lift my hand up to the top of the rug and push it down to my legs. Just thinking about all those actions is enough to exhaust me. Anyway, the weather's nice. I'm a grumpy old man. And in a little while the sun will go behind the nut tree and I'll be in the shade.

I left my glasses on my bedside table. I can see shapes and colours, blurring into each other. Blobs. An abstract painting, sort of. It's lovely. My memory still works well enough to be able to fill in the outlines and remember that over there is a wheelbarrow, and that's the box or the yew hedges, the row of spindle, the garden shed where I used to keep my tools.

I can't hear much anymore. It's quite pleasant. The noise of the town faded away a long time ago. I could easily pretend I was in the country. I miss the birdsong and the hum of insects, though. A blackbird has landed on the iron table right next to me. I can see from its open beak and the way its throat is vibrating that it's trilling away, but it's like a scene in a silent film. It's the same with the bees that come and go, like a never-ending ballet, to a spot on my rug where I must have dropped some jam yesterday. The blackbird flexes its claws, drops a green blob of shit on the table, and flies away.

You don't die in one go at my age. You're like a house whose shutters are being closed, whose furniture is being emptied out bit by bit, the gas cut off, then the water, and in the end the lights, before the door's locked one last time and the key thrown away. This thought amuses me. No-one can see me, but I'm smiling.

I'm not too warm now. I'm fine. I'm really fine. Doddery though I've become, my sense of smell is intact, and being able to smell the garden's scents makes me very happy. They're like a present that's been given to me for my last moments on earth. I've loved the earth. *To be on this earth.* As the expression goes, or the other one, *to come into the world.* To arrive. To pass over an infinitely wide surface. To land. To leave again. To disappear. The blackbird and its birdshit. The bees.

I don't care about time anymore. I don't try and find out what time it is anymore. I divide my day up the way I did when I was a child. Morning. Daytime. Evening. Night-time, when I sometimes leave my body and my age behind, when in my dreams I become the person I once was. Sometimes moments in the day even get mixed up with my dreams. It's a delicious feeling, not knowing anymore whether I'm dreaming or living, and even more delicious that it doesn't matter at all, it makes absolutely no difference.

Yesterday, yes, I think it was yesterday, unless it was a few minutes ago or maybe last week, I smelled the smell of the limes for the first time this spring. Their unsettling scent, intensified by the night's warmth. I suddenly thought about the adagio from Haydn's 61st symphony and the woman with brown hair. About her wet, warm sex, on that faraway May evening. My first woman's sex.

That prehistoric moment of my sex life. The thought affected me so strongly that I felt a tingling between my legs, yes, the same place where everything shut down a long time ago. But perhaps it was an illusion of tingling. Don't be a smartarse.

I never knew the name of the woman with brown hair. Not even her first name. I never knew anything about her and I never saw her again. I only heard her voice as a murmur. I only have the memory of her moans, of the cries she stifled by biting her lips, of her panting like a little animal – and all those sounds scaring me, making me think she was going to die in my arms, under the low branches of the blossoming limes, ringed by circling May bugs.

A few moments later, she vanished into the night and I collected up my clothes. In the distance I could make out the lights on the terrace of the *Biergarten* and hear the drinkers' laughter. Without my even noticing, the music from a little band of trombone, clarinet and bass drum, the players all in their green felt hats, had chased away the last notes of the student ensemble from the Academy of Music – to which my sister belonged – who, squeezed against each other in the bandstand that was too small for them all, had performed Haydn's beautiful symphony that evening.

I'm fifteen years old. I don't know anything about pleasure. People tell me I look older than my age. Every month, it feels like, my shirts and trousers shrink. My body stretches as if it was made of marshmallow, but I still see the world through a child's eyes. My mother spends her time unpicking hems and altering my father's clothes for me to wear. She opens his wardrobe, strokes the shirts and jackets and trousers. Picks up her scissors and needles. Cuts, sews and cries.

I wear a dead man's clothes. The war's been over for two years. My father never came back. An official document certifies that he's dead. My mother unfolds it many times a day. She keeps it in one of her pockets.

The town still looks like a huge set of teeth that someone smashed with a hammer. Stumps stick up in every street, black and crumbling. People have shovelled the rubble into huge heaps. Grass and weeds are starting to cover them with a layer of green. Bit by bit they're turning into hills. The trams are working again. They're crammed with lots more women than men. Or if they're men, they're old. Or they're half-men, missing an arm, a leg, both legs, both arms. Everyone's thin. Us too. We never eat our fill. Fortunately, there are books. And there's music. My sister plays the violin. She spent the whole war playing the violin. I spent it reading, and our mother spent it crying.

I wear a dead man's clothes but I don't remember him. I mean, at this moment, at the age of fifteen, I don't remember him anymore. Not a thing. Not his voice. Nor his height. Nor his hands. I don't even have any memory of missing him. Later, at odd moments in my life, I see him again. Specific scenes, glimpses that an internal machine has recorded in the bits of my brain that are hard to access and that it suddenly decides brutally to replay. My father, a cigarette between his fingers, points out to me a monkey grooming another monkey in a cage in the zoo. My father puts his arms around my mother in the kitchen and draws her into the staccato steps of a dance while the radio plays a tune I don't know. He is in his vest. It's summertime. My father on a bicycle, getting smaller as he cycles away, while I stay sitting on the steps of our building. He doesn't turn round but takes one hand off the handlebar to wave, as a goodbye.

I've never known what to do with these scenes. Nor

have I ever worked out why they used to pop into my head at odd moments. Moments that weren't crucial or particularly remarkable in my life.

My sister doesn't talk very much. She plays the violin. Endlessly. It's her way of expressing herself. She sleeps with her violin. The case is open by her bed. Depending on the light, it looks like a coffin or the wide-open mouth of some amphibious monster of the deep. The violin lies close to her face. Sometimes I watch them both sleeping. My sister has light-red hair. She's very beautiful. The violin is the colour of caramel.

I'm fifteen. I've read hundreds of books. I feel heavy with all these books, and the weight of them is marvellous. I'm going to carry on reading my whole life. I'm going to make it my job. I'll be a teacher. A special kind of teacher, who'll never teach, never have pupils, but will write books in which he'll talk about what he's read, to make others want and need to imitate him.

When my sister isn't playing her violin, she's reading scores. She doesn't realise that her fingers are moving as her eyes move over the notes, her lips too. Her violin lies on her knees. It makes me think of a pet waiting for someone to stroke it. Personally I've never learned how to read music. I don't have any desire to play music. Hearing it is enough for me.

My sister's three years older than me. She died at the end of the Fifties in a plane crash in South America. Several other players in the orchestra she was a member of also died. I've kept their tour programme: Mozart, Schubert, Brahms, Debussy. Twenty-nine dates are listed in it, in four different countries: Brazil, Argentina, Chile, Paraguay. Only the Brazil concerts took place and the first three dates in Argentina, at Buenos Aires. The plane never reached Mendoza.

Little by little my mother lost her mind. She ended her days in a psychiatric hospital. She died much later, after the wall came down, in a reunified country whose name didn't even mean anything to her anymore. For years when I came to visit her she would grasp my hands and keep hold of them, smile without recognising me, and murmur my father's name dozens and dozens of times. No other word ever left her lips.

The daylight's going. I feel fine. It's still warm, and I close my eyes. I don't know what time it might be. I don't know if Anne has arrived. Or left. I don't feel my aches and pains anymore. I don't feel my body. But here comes the smell of the limes again, wrapping itself around me like a shawl. Sugary. Sweet. Honeyed. I can feel that the woman with brown hair is going to come within reach, borne by this fleeting, powerful, magical scent.

I don't want to go to this concert. I'm stretched out on the green velvet sofa in the living room. I feel good there, like a cat. I'm reading *The Lily of the Valley*. I like French novelists. I think they're more sensitive than ours. I like the Russians too, but I keep out of my mother's way when I read them. Everything connected with Russia either sends her into a rage or crushes her, depending on her mood.

Félix de Vandenesse has distanced himself from Henriette de Mortsauf. He is having a feverishly passionate affair with Lady Dudley. He hears that Henriette is letting herself waste away. You're going to the concert. No. Do it for your sister. No. Please. I'm reading. Your book can wait. I won't go. Your sister's worried that not many people will come.

I leave Félix, grumbling to myself. I shut the book with a thump to show my displeasure. But I love my mother. I love my sister. My mother dresses me in a penguin suit. Without telling me, she has altered my father's wedding suit. It's black. The silk lapels shine. I put on a white shirt with a wing collar. My mother ties a bowtie around my neck. I feel ridiculous. The patent leather shoes are my size but much too smart. My mother tells me I'm very handsome. My sister agrees, smiling in the early evening light. She kisses my mother and leaves with her violin under her arm. My mother and I eat our tea. Potato soup and black bread, as always. My mother makes me put on an apron so I don't get any soup on the suit.

Out in the streets, which are still half-dead, people turn as I walk past. I've never felt so uncomfortable. Their looks weigh on me. I look as though I'm from a carefree pre-war era, as if I've sidestepped time's tunnel. I walk quickly. I pray the daylight will go and I'll disappear into the night.

The park is one of the few places in town that was spared by the war. Consistently for five years the bombs skirted it, probably because its hundred-year-old trees, its fishponds and little Japanese bridges, its flower beds full of perennials presented no danger. Or maybe it's just because death's capricious, striking when it wants, where it wants, not following any human logic.

Iron chairs have been arranged in concentric circles

around the bandstand. Many are still unfilled. I sit down on one, in the least well-lit place. The chairs around me are empty. I hope they'll stay empty. The orchestra's already in place, getting ready. My sister has seen me and makes a little nod in my direction. I nod back at her and squash myself as small as I can on my chair. There are about a hundred people in the audience. Shabbily dressed, the way everyone is in this period. In my expensive suit it feels as if I'm a prince who has suddenly appeared in their midst. I feel ashamed. The concert's about to start. The only light now is coming from inside the bandstand. The lights illuminate the musicians' faces, dusting them with gold. After some clearing of throats and the random notes of instruments being tuned one last time, the young conductor emerges from the darkness, runs up the three steps, bows to the applauding audience, waves, turns to the orchestra, raises his baton, and brings it down.

The notes lift into the May night sky. The audience is concentrating on listening. I breathe a bit more easily. No-one is paying attention to me anymore. I close my eyes. I listen to the symphony. I know it without knowing it. My sister has been practising her part for weeks. I know the melody, the rhythm, the way it develops. But at this moment it's as if someone has put flesh on a skeleton. I'm not merely discovering some bones that have been cleverly assembled, but a whole body in its marvellous complexity, supplemented by its flesh, covered with its skin, its hair, and alive.

The faint freshness that comes with the night makes the smells of warm earth, cut grass, humus, rose petals and slightly decaying wisteria rise from a thousand places in the park, and, as if encircling and surpassing them all, the smells of the tall limes and their dusty flowers. It feels as if the scents are intensified by Haydn's music, or they're extensions of it, creating a special echo made from some other matter to the melody. It's a long, marvellous moment. I forget my outfit and I forget Félix de Vandenesse. I'm inside the music and the park's springtime scents. The first movement comes to an end. Applause breaks the silence that follows the last note.

I open my eyes to applaud too, and to see my sister's happy face. I start. A woman is sitting on my right. She has sat down without my hearing her arrive. She's looking at me. She's not interested in the concert. Her body turned towards me, she's staring at me with her big dark eyes. Her face is very close to mine. I don't dare move. She has lovely long, brown, flowing hair. The second movement starts, and when it does the woman smiles at me and says a name, Viktor, as, with infinite slowness, her hand moves towards my cheek and, when it reaches it, strokes it with the back of her fingers. I'm petrified.

I pray for Anne to be late. For her bus not to have come. I feel so good. I want to remember again. To be fifteen again. To be in the park, by the bandstand, where my sister and her young friends are playing Haydn's music. My rug is keeping me beautifully warm. The evening's still a long way off. The scent of the limes keeps me company, like a faithful friend.

The brown-haired woman tirelessly repeats the name of Viktor as she strokes my face and her smiling eyes inspect it with astonishment, the way you do when you're reunited with a loved one you thought you'd lost for ever. She could be my mother's age. She's taller than her. Her worn clothes were once elegant. The material is expensive, though mended in places. She moves even closer to me. Her lips are next to my ear, in which she murmurs the name before kissing me. My heart beats wildly. Nobody is paying attention to us. We're the stuff of the night.

The first kiss is followed by another, then another. She holds my face between her hands and turns it towards hers. She comes even closer. Her lips brush mine. Viktor. Then press against them for a long time.

It's the first time anyone has kissed me like that. My eyes half-close. I discover how much the meeting of lips creates sweetness and confusion. Her fragile flesh brushes and presses against my own fragile flesh. Her warm breath mingles with mine. Then the tip of her tongue pushes my lips apart and slips into my mouth, bringing with it saliva that tastes of tobacco and strawberry ice cream, before snuggling up to my tongue and leading it on a slow circular journey. Unending and delicious.

I'll help you indoors. It's getting cooler. No, Anne, please. Leave me a bit longer. I'm with the woman with brown hair. Anne gives a little laugh. I keep my eyes shut. She knows. I've told her the story plenty of times. Where have you got to? She's just kissed me. Your ear? No, with her tongue. Already. Yes, but we're still sitting on our chairs. The concert's not over. It's the beautiful adagio. My son's my son, but he wouldn't understand any of this. And I've never dared talk to him about the woman with brown hair. Anne's not my son. She's a very kind-hearted woman. She doesn't judge me. She'd never think of calling me a mad old man. I'm going to get your tea ready. I'll come and get you in twenty minutes. Anne pulls up the rug, which has slipped a bit, adjusts the pillow under my head, and tenderly strokes the few hairs I have left, the way you stroke a baby's head. I hear her steps fade away on the gravel.

The woman with brown hair is there again, as close as a person can be. I can feel her body against mine. I feel drunk but I've never known what it's like to be drunk. Her hands are stroking my suit, then opening my jacket, flattening themselves against my shirt, undoing three buttons, pressing against my skin, sliding over it. I'm no longer breathing. I'm going to die. I'm fifteen and I'm going to die, with the sound of Haydn's music in the background, among the swirling scent of the limes.

Without realising it, I've put my arms around the woman with brown hair. At this she shuts her eyes and throws her head back. I plunge my head into the place below her neck and kiss her. My kisses rain down between her breasts, which are burning through the thin material. She takes my hands and guides them to her hips, to the hollow below her stomach. There opens up the landscape of abundance and of treasure islands.

Afterwards I try to find the woman with brown hair. I come to the park on many following evenings, in every season. I go to numerous concerts, never missing those with Haydn in their programme. The years pass without my ever seeing her again. I don't know whether her madness has ended up carrying her far beyond our human world. Whether she has died from too great a lack of love. Whether she has ended up throwing herself off a bridge or into a river, consumed by the pain of having lost Viktor for ever. Time cannot alter, even in the slightest way, the memory I have of her, and though I'm forever grateful to her for my first experience of sexual passion, above all I owe her my love of women.

The symphony's third movement accompanies us to the beckoning velvet darkness of the tall limes. We aren't in real life anymore. We have walked into a dream. The music gives the dream a deep, cosy quality. For millennia, men have believed that sometimes gods have conjoined with mortal women, or that men have been visited by the tributes of goddesses. On this May evening I experience my own mythology.

We have lain down on the grass. Our eyes seek each other's in the obscurity. Our pupils are stars, tossed into the high May sky. I'm not fifteen. I'm not fifteen anymore. It doesn't mean anything. Time doesn't exist. It's a shabby invention of book-keepers. Gently, the woman with brown hair undresses me, then I undress her. Naked, we cling tightly to each other. Her skin smells of lime blossom. I am a faun. My cock gets hard. It frightens and thrills me. She cradles both hands around it, the way you hold a candle when you're afraid its flame might go out. I slide my fingers between her opened thighs. It's all burning and crystal-clear there. She guides me into her. My god, that first time. I feel as though I'm falling from a clifftop without fearing I'll ever hit the ground. The air around my falling body envelops and intoxicates me. It keeps going.

Fourth and last movement. *Prestissimo.*

Where have you been? Your sister's been home for a long time. She looked for you everywhere. And look at your suit. My god, what a state! You'll be the death of me.

My mother is waiting for me in the hallway of our building. Her face is lined with worry. She has lost a husband. She doesn't want to lose a son. I don't say anything in reply. What could I say? I go upstairs to bed.

I stay in my room in silence for two days. My mother brings me infusions. My sister, at my request, plays me Haydn's adagio each evening. They both think I'm ill. I just want to make my dream last longer. On my fingers I still have the scent of the sex of the woman with brown hair and the memory of her bush. I breathe in the smell. I am back under the limes. I'm back inside her. I'm lovesick.

You must come in now. What? You must come in. Look, you can't see a thing anymore and you'll catch your death. It's death that'll catch me, Anne, and quicker than you think. Don't say silly things. Come on. I'll help you. You smell of the limes. Anne helps me get up off the lounger. It takes us for ever. It's cold suddenly. My carcass is like a crushed chicken's. I hurt everywhere. Can you smell the scent, Anne? No. What scent? What are you talking about? I can only smell the exhaust fumes of the cars, and the noise of the trams is giving me a headache. We walk at a snail's pace. Come on, dear man. The garden is black. The house is far away. Too far. I'd like to stay in the garden and fall asleep there. You're mad.

My fifteenth birthday is a long way away. My life is a long way away. The woman with brown hair is a long way away.

When my son was born I called him Viktor. My wife asked me why. I lied. I said it was a fine name. A name that meant victory. That our son was going to be victorious. It was all ridiculous. But I couldn't tell the truth. I couldn't say about the woman with brown hair, her sex open like a smile, her dead love, the limes, Haydn. The park and its trees spared by the war.

I've had a happy life. A loving wife who I loved back. A son who's a son. I'm going to die without regrets. You're not going to die. Of course I am. I don't think I've done wrong, and if I have, I didn't mean to. When I felt my semen spurt inside the sex of the woman with brown hair on that May evening, under the leaves of the limes, and I heard her cries of love, her moans like a wounded animal, her sighs, her gasps, I felt I was being wrenched from myself. Afterwards, I don't know if I ever came back to myself. Is that what marks the end of adolescence? That violent entry into the adult world. That pleasure, of such an intensity you can only feel it at the cost of the vivid sadness that follows it. And of the days of regret afterwards. The infinite days of regret.

You're saying things that are too complicated for me. You're talking like a book. I don't understand a word. Anne pours potato soup into my bowl. She cuts a slice of coarse black bread. Why don't you want me to make you something else to eat? A meal that would fill you up. With meat, with a sauce. With cream. At your age, that's what you need. At my age. You know what I need, you who know nothing. I know this soup is going to kill you. There's nothing in it. It's just water.

Anne, dear Anne, for goodness' sake let me eat as though I'm fifteen. The ghosts are there. By the door. You don't see them but they're there. The ones I love. They're there. They're watching us and you don't see them. What are you going on about now? You're too young, you've got time. Each day their shapes are more clearly outlined to me. It thrills me. I'm going to be one of them. You can't understand. Soon they'll take me in their misty arms. I'll feel their hearts beating to the non-existent rhythm of eternity. At least eat your soup. It's getting cold. And stop talking to me about ghosts, I shan't be able to sleep tonight. There'll also be the smell of lime blossom for ever, the beautiful adagio from the bandstand, the blazing embrace of the sex of the woman with brown hair around my boyish cock. Be quiet, you mad old man. You're right, I'm nothing but a mad old man, a mad old man of fifteen.

That's how life ends its final chapter, Anne: everything's summed up and joined up. I'm going to go to sleep and live at last. It'll be a long evening in May. There'll be young people full of promise, who'll be playing a symphony in the lovely park of a town in ruins. After the war. After all wars. And as I listen to them, waiting under the tall trees for a person who is very special in my life, I won't have to close my eyes anymore, you see, because they'll be wide open for ever.

IRMA GRESE

IT WAS THE MAYOR WHO HAD INSISTED. A GOOD girl. Irma. Irma Grese. Who's never been given a chance. Not very bright but not a bad girl. A difficult family. She deserves a helping hand. The manager let herself be convinced. In any case, she hardly had a say in the matter, the retirement home depended on council funding. She herself had been recruited by the mayor. How could she refuse? The elections were coming. The town was handing out as many public sector jobs as it was Christmas parcels for the elderly. The mother had told her daughter to go and see the mayor. To ask for something. Anything. Be on your best behaviour. Maybe he'll have a job.

The two Germanys were only one now, as they had

been for the last five years. The communists had become liberals, but the poor had stayed poor. It was hard to understand a lot of it.

The girl was seventeen. Never looked the person who was speaking to her in the eyes. She gave the impression of living in a permanent daze. A big stupefied face with cheeks that were too pink, nearly raw. Eyes that were too blue. A forehead that was too low. Neither ugly nor beautiful. Limbs that were too heavy. Hair too fine. So blonde it was nearly white.

Her CV took up three lines. She had gone to school till she was thirteen. Then stopped. Why? She had shrugged. The manager had asked her again. The mayor was still there. The girl had eventually said her mother had needed her. To help her. Her little brothers. Her little sisters. They popped out of their mother regularly. And never a father in her world, or rather plenty of fathers. When the manager asked her what she knew how to do, she shrugged again. A bit of everything. Not much.

She could feed the ones who can't feed themselves anymore. It was the mayor who had spoken. She's done that with her brothers and sisters. She could do it with the old people. Listen. With my father, for instance. You say he'll need someone at every meal. That it's becoming almost impossible.

The manager nodded. Why not. We can do that. Yes. And a bit of cleaning too. That'll make a full-time job. Three months' trial. Perfect. The mayor stood up. The girl didn't know what she was supposed to do. Stand up or stay where she was. The manager saw the mayor out and came back to her office. The girl hadn't moved. Slumped on her chair, like a joint of meat someone had put down. She was wearing cheap jeans. A T-shirt that was too small and showed the bulges of her hips rolling over the top of her jeans. A tattoo was visible on the back of her neck. An ideogram. What does that mean? the manager asked, to be friendly. The girl shrugged. Dunno. It's Chinese.

The manager showed her round the home. The staff locker rooms. The kitchens. The big residents' lounge. The dining room. The TV room. The two treatment rooms. The garden. Three paths for walks. A terrace. Four tables. Chairs. And then the two floors of residents' rooms. Wheelchairs parked everywhere, as if they had been arranged in an arcane order for some strange role-play game, and in each of them old, immobile bodies secured in place by a cloth belt knotted across their stomach, with crumpled faces: you couldn't always tell whether the face belonged to a man or a woman.

The manager greeted them cheerfully, calling them by their names. Some responded. Most made do with slowly lifting their blank gaze to her and moving their lips without any sound coming out. Some did not even react.

The girl followed the manager like an animal. She thought there were a lot of old people. Way too many old people. What were they waiting for? What were they for? Did they really need to be around, taking up so much room? There was that smell too. Soup and dirty nappies. She didn't like this place. Will you be alright? the manager asked her. The girl shrugged and said yes. I'll introduce you to the mayor's father. It's here. Room 104.

The manager knocked with three cheerful little knocks. They entered. The room had the same smell as the corridors, just worse. Because everything was shut. Near the window was an armchair, identical to all the other armchairs. In the armchair was an old man who looked like the mayor. A thinner version. Greyer. More slumped. A thirty years older version.

Hello Viktor! How are we today? the manager asked,

putting a hand on his shoulder. The old man looked at her. Something like a smile appeared in his eyes, but went out almost immediately.

I want to introduce you to your new guardian angel! This young lady is going to make a fuss of you. She's going to help you with your meals. Isn't she kind?

The old man's almost dead eyes turned to the girl. Again a smile seemed to light up in them and then ebbed away as if the effort really was too great.

I'll let you get to know each other. Come back to my office afterwards to sign your contract.

No signs of the old man's life were visible in the room. It was as if he'd just found himself there in transit. No clothes. No magazines. The bed made immaculately. Bare walls. Yellow and blue. Emptiness. On his bedside table, no vase or pot plant, just a glass filled with water and in the water a set of dentures.

A door led to the bathroom. A shower with a seat. A toilet. A washbasin. A bathroom cabinet. She pushed her jeans down, then her knickers. Sat on the bowl, which was very tall. She took her time.

She came back into the bedroom. The old man followed her with his eyes. She didn't look at him. Behaved as if he didn't exist. She opened the cupboard. Four pairs of underpants. Socks. A pair of trousers. Three shirts. Two waistcoats. A satchel. Inside it a wallet. Identity papers. Driving licence. Voter's card. A very old black-and-white photo which showed a group of smiling soldiers holding dogs on leads in front of some wagons. Three ten-Deutschmark notes. Three one-mark coins. She hesitated. Left them. Shut the cupboard.

She sat on the bed. The old man moaned or tried to say something. She ignored him. She looked out of the window. You could see trees, roofs and the top of the illuminated sign at Apokalypse, a bar that had dancing at night. It belonged to a guy from Munich. A guy from the West who looked like all the guys from the West, who drove round in a big Mercedes with tinted windows, had bought half the town and looked down on them as if they were all peasants.

She could happily have spent her life at Apokalypse. But for that you had to have money. In reality she hardly went there. Music. Dancing. She loved dancing. That's not going to put food on your plate! her mother told her. She shrugged. She went on dancing in her bed-room. Music at full volume. Brothers and sisters, who squabbled next door, who cried and whined. Who were hungry. Sleepy. Thirsty.

Did that go alright? She pouted in a way that could mean yes. You'll see, the mayor's father isn't difficult. Don't be surprised if he sometimes hums old military tunes. Let him do it. He's not hurting anyone. The war left its mark on him. I mean, he paid a price. Everyone made mistakes. Especially then. He has a right to a happy old age. What was she talking about? She didn't understand anything the manager was saying. The war, it was the Middle Ages to her.

She signed the contract by writing out her name. Tracing the letters the way an eight-year-old does. Big and shaky. It took time. With her pointy tongue between her lips, under the gaze of the manager who didn't know quite what to make of this girl. She told her she would start next morning, at seven. She opened her eyes and mouth wide. Seven? she repeated incredulously. The manager nodded. Yes. Seven o'clock.

She had a really hard time getting up. She was the first one up in the house. She drank a glass of cold milk. Put her clothes on without washing herself. No time. Didn't want to. Her mother was still in bed. Brothers and sisters too. She saw the morning world. It hadn't happened to her in a long time. People hurrying. Running to get to work. Mad people. With crumpled faces. She was one of them now.

When she got to the retirement home, the manager was waiting for her. She commented that she was five minutes late. Five minutes late on her first day. It wasn't a good start. What difference did five minutes make? Five minutes didn't matter to old people. They had all the time in the world. She didn't answer.

The manager went with her to the kitchens. She showed her how to make the breakfast tray for the mayor's father: coffee with milk, two slices of bread with butter and jam. A yoghurt. An apple purée. He must eat it all. I mean all. Slowly. Then you wait for a little while and take him for a bowel movement. For a what? To the toilet if you prefer. You put him on the toilet. You go out. You wait. What do I wait for? What do you think? She understood and retched. And what do I do afterwards? You wipe him. I wipe him? You wipe him. You dress him again. You take him back to his armchair.

She looked at the floor. Beige tiles, grey mortar. She made a disgusted face. Will you be alright? the manager asked. The girl shrugged. I'll leave you. You need to go to him now.

The old man had been got out of bed, washed and dressed. He was waiting for her seated in the armchair pushed up to a small table. She put the tray down on it. He followed her with his eyes. She didn't say hello to him. What was the point. They had explained to her that he had lost the power of speech. That he might not have all his faculties. He must be deaf too.

She put the tray down. Sat facing him. Picked up a slice of bread and lifted it to his mouth. He opened it. His eyes gleamed. His dentures closed on the bread. She pulled. The old man tore off a piece, started chewing it. It was slow. He chewed. He grunted and dribbled. Made horrible noises, like squeezing a sponge and sniffing. Eventually he succeeded in swallowing. She brought the slice of bread to his mouth again. He snatched it like a tortoise she had had when she was a little girl, which she had fed with lettuce leaves. It took him ten minutes to eat the first slice of bread.

Then she picked up the bowl of milky coffee, which had already cooled down, and held it to his lips. Half of it ran down his chin and neck onto the bib. She tried again. The old man gurgled. She started with the second slice of bread. It was endless. It felt like being punished. To think she could be doing something else. Be somewhere else. Sleeping. There was still the yoghurt and the purée. With a teaspoon. Teaspoon after teaspoon. An eternity. The old man's face lit up when she started with the purée. He must like it. He was making little sounds. Like an excited rodent. His lips were smeared with jam, butter, milky coffee, yoghurt and purée. He looked like a very old baby, wrinkled and horrible. She wiped him with the bib.

The old man was looking at her. His thin head wobbled without stopping. It looked as if it was mounted on a spring. She pushed the table aside, grasped him under his arms, and pulled him roughly out of his chair. Standing, he was a head shorter than her. Holding him up, she led him to the bathroom. He moved forwards like a Japanese robot, sliding his feet across the floor, all of it with a doddering slowness, as if his battery had run down.

He stopped next to the toilet and turned round. She unfastened the belt of his trousers, unbuttoned them, unzipped his flies. The trousers fell down on their own. Oversized white underpants appeared, from which emerged two wasted chicken's thighs, white and hairless. She turned away, pulled down the underpants and sat the old man on the seat. She went back into the bedroom, sat on the bed. Looked out of the window. The trees. The roofs. The sign at Apokalypse. Waited for half an hour.

She went back to the bathroom. The old man had nodded off on the toilet. He was snoring. She flushed it. That woke him. The noise and then the water splashing his backside. She stood him up. Averted her gaze, pulled up his underpants, his trousers. Buttons. Flies. Belt. Put him back in his armchair. Pushed him next to the window. Picked up the breakfast tray. Took it back down to the kitchens.

Now you can wash the two corridors downstairs. Then this afternoon you'll do the two upstairs. That will make up your hours. She was given two buckets, a scrubbing brush, a mop and cleaning products, all on a trolley. What did they think she was? A skivvy? She swallowed her protests, pushed her trolley. Attacked the first corridor. She cleaned it in a rage, on all fours, filled with a violent energy that attracted the admiration of three old women whose armchairs were lined up at an angle next to each other and who looked like sisters with their faded blouses and their purple hair and their droopy cow's ears. What a good girl, one said. And determined, the second said. And pretty with it, the third added, whose spectacles hung at the end of a gilded chain.

She didn't look in their direction or say a word. She moved on to the second ground-floor corridor. She had only just finished scrubbing when an old guy went past in his electric wheelchair with a zizzing noise like a coffee machine. He had come in from the garden. He left two long parallel tracks on the damp floor, glistening and spotted with muddy earth. She could have killed him.

It was already time to go to the kitchens and make up the tray for the old man's lunch. The cook was a Turk of about forty, dark-skinned and thin. He had a big mouth, two gold teeth, and tattoos of mermaids on his hands. She had seen him at Apokalypse. Always with a girl glued to him. When she had the tray in her hands, grated carrots, minced beef, peas, pear in syrup, he took advantage of her hands being full to stroke her bum. I'll throw this in your face if you don't stop that. Go ahead and try, he said to her, smiling. You're a dick, she said after a pause, smiling too. The cook's hands made her feel all hot inside. His name was Özek.

The old man hadn't moved from the window. Between being like that and being dead, she couldn't see the difference. What could be the use of staying alive like that? She put the tray down. The bib on. Held out the first forkful of carrots. It was like the morning all over again.

Except this time it lasted twice as long. She couldn't bear it. It was hard for the old man to swallow. He kept it all in his mouth. She got him to drink some water but it didn't help. He stored the food like a hamster. It looked like he had a ping-pong ball in each cheek. She pressed them.

The old man seemed to understand. He rolled anxious eyes and attempted to swallow, but only managed to choke and spit out on the bib half of what he had in his mouth. She told him off. She wiped the bib with a tissue, threw it in the toilet. We're going to make an effort now!

The old man swallowed the mince at military speed, along with the gulps of water she gave him between mouthfuls. But he refused to open his lips when she held out a spoonful of peas. She tried to force a way in, but it was no use. Just doing it to piss me off, is that it?

He looked at the pear in syrup with a gleam of desire, though. She understood. She cut a chunk of the pear in the ramekin, added juice to the spoon and held it out to the old man, whose mouth opened immediately. Too easy! She withdrew the spoon. No peas, no pear, that'll teach you! She tipped the pear into the plate of peas. Stood up. Went and threw the lot in the toilet. Flushed it. The old man watched her do it, his eyes wide open with sadness. She dragged him upright and pulled him to the bathroom, undressed him, put him on the toilet. Shut the door. Sat on the bed.

The trees. The roofs. The sign at Apokalypse. The cook's hand on her bum. His hand with its mermaids. The heat she'd felt. She had an urge to play with herself. She didn't dare. Not on the bed. Not in the old man's room. Suppose someone came in. The manager. A nurse.

She went to get the old man. Pulled his underpants and trousers back up. Flushed the toilet. Dragged him over to the bed. For a siesta. And then you can leave him. You lower the shutters a bit. That's all.

It was her break. She had a right to it. It was

lunchtime, but she wasn't hungry. She went outside. Behind the building where the kitchens were. Two chairs. An ashtray on the ledge of a low window. She got out her Walkman and her headphones and turned on the music. Full volume. The beat. Nothing but the beat. Simple. Crude. She smoked two cigarettes. Her head was empty of thoughts. The music filled her up. She kept her eyes closed, her face turned towards the sun. She felt okay. She forgot the old man. The sun went behind a cloud. She opened her eyes. It wasn't a cloud, the cook was in front of her, lighting a cigarette and looking at her in a way she knew, with a smile she knew, which gave her shivers in her stomach. He was talking to her but she couldn't hear anything. She took off her headphones.

How old are you? Eighteen, she lied. Eighteen, that's good. You? she asked. Thirty-seven. You're old. Old's good. Old knows. What does old know? You want me to show you? She shrugged. Stubbed out her cigarette. It was time for the corridors. I have to go. He stood across the doorway. Get out the way. Go on, you can pass. Get out the way. Get me out of the way then. She pushed him aside. Felt his snake-like body against her hand.

Shrugged. Smiled. He stroked her cheek and her breasts.

When she started cleaning the upstairs corridors, a great feeling of tiredness overcame her. Not used to scrubbing like this. So long. So hard. And not understanding why either. It was all clean. The corridors were deserted at this time. The old people were in their bedrooms or outside, in the shade, in the garden. Some were in front of the TV too, in the residents' lounge. Dozing.

Is everything alright? She hadn't heard her coming. The manager was behind her. Huge. Standing over her. And her on all fours. She shrugged. Yes. The manager glanced at her watch. At five-thirty don't forget to make up the tray. I'll let you get on. That's right, let me get on. Go back to your office. Go back to your cushy job.

She washed the two corridors. Watched the floors dry, not thinking. Then she took the cleaning things back down, put them away. Went and smoked a cigarette. She could hear the cook singing in the kitchens but couldn't see him. Soup smells wafted from a window. She hated soup. Had done since she was tiny. Time wouldn't pass. Time had never passed. When would she finally be able to get away? To get on with her life? Her own, not her stupid mother's.

When she saw the tea that had been made for the old man, she told herself it would go quicker. Soup. Mashed ham. Mashed potatoes. Custard. All soft.

He didn't react when she entered. He was in the same place. In the armchair. Facing the window. Eyes closed. Maybe he was dead. She put the tray down on the table, making a noise. He didn't open his eyes. His head had flopped onto his chest. She shook him with her fingertips. He raised his head, opened his eyes, saw her. Looked at the tray blankly. Looked back at her. She unfolded the bib, tied it round his neck. And everything began again. The slowness. The spoonfuls. The mouthfuls. The food stored in his cheeks. A torment. A torture. Not to mention that she was starting to get hungry. She ate the slice of bread. Then the custard. If you'd been a bit quicker. It was nearly six-thirty. She threw the rest of the soup, mash and ham down the toilet, flushed it and put the old man on the seat. It wasn't her business anymore. She'd finished her day. It was other people's business now.

So? her mother asked when she got home. So what?

What was it like? She shrugged. Look after your brothers. The fuck are you talking about? What? I've been working all day. And you think I've been twiddling my thumbs? She dashed to her room, locked the door, and turned her music on full. The bass silenced her mother's shouts. She danced. She danced for an hour. Not thinking about a thing. Then thinking about the cook's hands. The blue drawings of mermaids.

Next day she arrived on time. The manager congratulated her on her punctuality. She went to the kitchens. Didn't see the cook, he must get there later or be busy somewhere else. She made a bowl of coffee, fetched milk, two slices of bread. Yoghurt. Purée. Put it all on a tray. Went up to the old man's room.

The room smelled of night. A urine and warm animal smell. The bed had been made but no-one had aired the room. The old man was already washed, dressed, sitting on the chair near the window. He was crooning. "*Die Fahne hoch! Die Reihen dicht geschlossen. SA marschiert mit ruhig festen Schritt.*"[1] It seemed to excite him. He tapped

[1] "Flags held high! Ranks closed tight. The SA marches with calm firm step." Words from the "Horst-Wessel-Lied", the song that was the anthem of the SA (*Sturmabteilung*), the Nazi Party's original paramilitary wing, then of the Nazi Party itself.

time with one foot. She didn't know his song. She went over to him without a word, put the tray on the table, knotted his bib around his neck. He stopped singing. It was only the second day, but she already felt as if she was repeating the same gestures for the thousandth time. She opened the window. It had started raining. Blackbirds sang as they hopped across the lawn.

She started feeding the old man. It was like the day before. Slow. Desperate. She was already fed up with him. And she was hungry too. She'd had time to have a shower, but not to eat anything. The old man stopped at the second slice of bread. She ate the purée. Then the yoghurt. He watched her. He had suddenly stopped chewing. What? What difference does it make? You wouldn't have eaten them anyway. Would you? And doing it this way we don't waste time. Come on, potty time! She pulled him to the bathroom. Pulled down his trousers, underpants, sat him on the toilet. Left him with the uneaten slice of bread in his hand. You finish it! You have to finish. I don't want to see anything in your hand when I come back.

She went out and sat down on the bed. Yawned.

Afterwards it was buckets of water, corridors, lunch, more corridors, tea.

Always the same.

Like that.

Every day.

And in the evening her mother, giving her grief about nothing and everything.

The only times when there was any variety were her breaks. Smoking a cigarette or two outside. Or letting herself be caressed by the cook when he was there. When they were alone. He would pull her into the storeroom. He'd stroke her lightly with his mermaid hands. He'd touch her breasts under her T-shirt, pull down her knickers. He talked to her in the language of his country. Usually she didn't like Turks, strangers, Muslims. They stole the work of real Germans. It was because of people like them she was in the shit. But him, it wasn't the same. When he pushed his fingers inside her, she got all wet and moaned. He had long, fine fingers that burned her.

That was how the first week went. Like being dead for a hundred years. With a few sunny intervals. She couldn't stand the old man anymore. She could have been somewhere else. Asleep in her bed. Dancing. Hanging around Apokalypse. Smoking fags with the cook. Kissing him.

Being stroked. Instead, she was holding out forkfuls of mashed potato.

And there were more weeks. She started to hate him. It was as if the old man was stealing her time, her youth. He was her punishment. She could have done so many other things if he hadn't been there. His slowness drove her mad. And his smell. His stupid song. Always the same one. That he hummed on repeat. The colour of his skin. His big wet eyes. His whole head wobbling. His thin, knotty hands whose blue, swollen veins wriggled like worms. He was repulsive. Useless. You didn't even know what was going on in his head. Or even if he had anything going on in his head. Maybe it had become completely hollow, like those shells of dead snails you found in the garden at the end of winter that you stamped on.

She couldn't be bothered to get him to swallow his whole meal anymore. She ate half, or three quarters, or all of it, depending on whether she was hungry, whether she liked the food or not. It was the cook who made the dishes. Eating them, she thought of his hands, his skin, his cock which he had slipped into her one evening, in the storeroom. It was the first time. It had hurt her.

She'd bled. At the same time it had shaken her to her core. You like that. Yes, she'd said. The food made her feel closer to him. When she wasn't very hungry, after she'd given the old man two or three mouthfuls, she threw the rest down the toilet. Flushed it. Put the old man on the toilet seat. Left him there for half an hour.

As the days passed, he started to waste away. He spent hours dozing, in a state of semi-consciousness. His neck looked like the neck of a baby bird in its nest, when it has no down and all you can see is red flesh barely covered by a film of fragile, translucent skin. Feverish skin.

Is he eating well? Yes. Does he eat everything? Yes. The manager looked at the mayor's father. The girl was next to her. Yet he's much thinner. The girl shrugged. The old man had his eyes closed. His head on his chest. He snored gently.

The doctor came and listened to his chest. Anaemia. Old age. Nothing out of the ordinary, all in all. He was put on a drip. The girl watched the solution drip through. Are you happy? You want to get me sacked, do you? She hated him even more. She finished the celery salad. Attacked the chicken breast. She enjoyed making little chunks dance in front of his eyes. He opened his mouth. His eyes gleamed with desire. The effort made him tremble. She moved the chunk away. Popped it in her mouth. That's good. It's so good, chicken. It amused her. The old man didn't have the strength to shout but his look begged her. She refused to feel sorry. She finished lunch. Burped. Took the old man to the toilet. Left him there. Stretched out on the bed.

When she was washing the corridors she thought about the cook. She imagined him coming up behind her. When she was on all fours. He had taken her like that once in the storeroom. That made her think of the dogs in the photo in the old man's wallet, which she'd looked at closely when she'd finally taken the ten-Deutschmark notes. Well, what would he have done with them? The old man must have been one of those soldiers. The one on the far left. She recognised his big ears. There was a guy in front of them too, very thin, in a funny striped suit and who was on all fours as if he was a dog too. He was the one the soldiers were looking at. And he was the one making them laugh. But the guy wasn't laughing.

The day went quicker when she thought about the

cook. They made love every evening. When she went and took back the old man's tray. It was good to feel him inside her. Are you taking precautions? Yes, she lied. That's good. She kissed his mermaid hands.

The doctor couldn't understand. Despite the drip. Despite the meals. The old man was slipping away.

The mayor was informed.

She found him in the room one day, sitting next to the old man. She came in with the tray. Come in. Come in. She put the tray down on the table, by the bed. The old man was lying down. His eyes closed.

It's the end, the mayor said. He's had a long life. We all end up like this, he added. She thought, Not me. I'm not going to end up like that. I've got plenty of time. I'm seventeen.

Thank you for what you've done, the mayor went on. She didn't understand him. It's nice of you to look after old people. You're a good girl. She shrugged. The old man let out a long wheeze, as if he had searched every corner of his lungs to find a bit of air. Do you mind leaving us? I need to be alone with him. She picked up the tray. Went out of the room. Back down to the kitchen. She wasn't quite sure what she should do. She fetched the trolley, the scrubbing brush, the bucket, the cleaning products, the mop. She started cleaning the corridors.

The old man died at the end of the day.

She found out next morning.

I don't quite know what I'm going to do with you. The manager was thoughtful. She had called her into her office. She looked at the girl standing in front of her, looking at the floor, twisting and turning her fat fingers. The mayor's very kind, but now his father's left us, I don't have enough work for you. Do you understand? Do you understand what I'm saying? The girl shrugged. She said yes because she felt the manager was waiting for an answer.

That's the spirit. You're young. I'll write you a reference.

She went home at lunchtime. Have you been kicked out? No. Have you done something stupid? No. What am I going to do with you? Her mother, in her dressing gown, shook her head. The girl shrugged. Anyway, it was a shitty job.

She went to her room. Put her music on at full volume. She wanted to dance, but suddenly she felt she was going to be sick. She lay down on her bed. It went away.

She lit a cigarette. She thought about the old man again. His head like a mummy's. His mouth. She chased the image away with another one, of the cook's hands. His mermaid tattoos. His fingers, wiry and gentle at the same time. His brown, taut skin. She told herself she'd go to Apokalypse that evening. That she was free. That she didn't have to watch a clock anymore. That tomorrow she could sleep till lunchtime. That nobody could give her orders anymore. That she could do what she wanted with her life from now on.

She was seven weeks pregnant.

She didn't know it yet.

GNADENTOD

Unpublished drawings by Franz Marc
to be auctioned

On 26 May, at the famous Drouot auction house in Paris, the sale will take place of around forty drawings by Franz Marc (1880–1940), today considered one of the greatest artists of the first half of the twentieth century. Marc was murdered by the Nazi authorities in what has come to be known as Aktion T4, during which approximately 80,000 physically and mentally disabled people, and other residents of psychiatric institutions, were gassed. For Elisabeth John, a specialist in the work of Franz Marc, and the expert appointed for the sale being organised by the auctioneer Tajan, "there is no doubt that these drawings are the work of the creator of the *Blaue Reiter*". She adds that they represent "a profound discovery in the work of Marc: dated as they are to 1937, the drawings prove that the artist, contrary to what had always been thought, had not given up making art after the First World War". The sale price estimate for the drawings, whose subjects are mostly wolves and dogs, is 90,000 euros.

Article by D. K.

in *Frankfurter Allgemeine Zeitung*,

16 May 2004

File no. 21-AG-3206
Franz Moritz Wilhelm Marc
Note FM 7140 3KTE

On this day, 7 January 1940, the Committee of Enquiry of Public Health for the Assessment of Patients has been requested to consider the case of Franz Moritz Wilhelm Marc, German citizen, born 8 February 1880 in Munich. The subject, 60 years old, has been held in the public institution of Eglfing-Haar since August 1923, making him its longest-standing inmate.

His file indicates that he had previously spent three periods of differing lengths in other psychiatric hospitals, the first following an arrest in a Berlin street on 5 May 1920 for a public order offence. The police report indicates that the subject had climbed onto a bench in the Kirschenstrasse and had gradually undressed, folding his clothes as he went and balancing them on his head until he was entirely naked. He did not say anything and did not resist when the police came to interrupt his performance.

He remained completely mute throughout his subsequent interrogation, and it quickly became apparent that his case was a psychiatric one. He was referred to Doctor Schnigge of the P. B. Schotz institute, who diagnosed advanced schizophrenic delirium of catatonic type and recommended immediate internment. His wife, Maria Marc, gave her consent. The subject spent five months at Doctor Schnigge's institute, where he received electric shock treatment which bore some fruit: the subject was declared fit for discharge from the institution by doctors in mid-October 1920.

Franz Marc's file indicates that he then presented himself of his own volition at the doors of the institute in the first days of March 1921. His wife was unaware of his decision. He gave no motive for it and remained silent in the face of the doctors' questioning. Doctor Willart, the successor to Doctor Schnigge who had died in December 1920, made the decision to intern the subject. This time his stay lasted about a year. The doctors continued the electric shock treatment, which he tolerated well. He suffered no further breakdown, and it was decided once more to bring his stay at the institute to an end.

Marc left the institute on 3 February 1922. It seems likely that he returned to live with his wife, who had moved to Munich where she continues to reside.

In the summer of 1923, several police reports mention minor incidents in which Franz Marc was implicated. All of them took place in the Englischer Garten in Munich, specifically in the location of the Chinese tower. According to eyewitness statements, Franz Marc was found crawling across the lawn, slowly and cautiously, like a soldier preparing to attack, in the direction of holiday-makers who were sitting in the Biergarten. He showed no signs of violence whatsoever, but his behaviour eventually frightened the children and annoyed members of the public. Park keepers called the police. Franz Marc offered no resistance at the time of his arrest on 5 August 1923. His wife signed a consent form for his admission to the psychiatric asylum at Eglfing-Haar, where he has resided since that time.

Over the following years Franz Marc was subjected to further electric shock therapies, but these were abandoned when doctors realised the patient was in no danger of a breakdown that posed a risk to himself or to others. Compliant and placid, mute at all times, he was employed as time went on in a number of different tasks within the asylum, carrying out conscientiously the jobs he was entrusted with: gardening, washing floors, toilets and washrooms, making paper bags, peeling vegetables. The reports mention a single refusal that took place when staff wanted Franz Marc to carry out some painting tasks in a dormitory which was being redecorated. He threw the brushes he had been given onto the floor and tipped over the pots of paint.

This was felt to be even more surprising because Franz Marc, a painter's son, had himself studied painting at Munich's Academy of Fine Arts and had pursued a career as an artist up till the Great War, enjoying a certain success among the debased and corrupt society that we have since known to be so heavily responsible for the disaster of the defeat. But the trauma of war doubtless acted upon him as a revelation, allowing him to reject forcefully the siren call of an art that could lead nowhere, in the sense that it was merely lies and a catalyst to degeneracy.

It is in this context illuminating to read the report written by Doctor Gästner following the visit he made on 28 July 1937, with a number of the institute's calmest patients, including Franz Marc, to the enlightening exhibition "*Entartete Kunst*"[2] which had opened to the public in the Institute of Archaeology building that month. Among the works on display were paintings by Franz Marc himself. Doctor Gästner noted that, when he led the subject to these pictures to observe his reactions, Franz Marc showed no emotion or feelings whatsoever. When the doctor showed the patient that it was he who had once painted these pictures, the latter still gave no reaction and walked off.

Later that same morning, when the little group visited the Haus der Deutschen Kunst located opposite the exhibition, Doctor Gästner noted that the behaviour of Franz Marc changed and that the patient seemed to show a great interest in the works that were on show there, bearing witness to German genius. He noticed in particular that the subject lingered for an extended moment in front of the masterpiece *The Four Elements*

2 "Degenerate Art".

by Adolf Ziegler, which belongs to our Führer, who had been generous in lending it so that visitors could enjoy it.

"The patient's features were transformed," Doctor Gästner writes. "A smile appeared on his face, which was something I had never observed before, as he never deviated from a constant expression of absence and stupefaction. Doubtless within his confused mind he had managed, despite everything, to be moved by the force and grandeur of the work, which would tend to prove that when art attains a high point of excellence and clothes itself in enlightening virtues, it can succeed in reaching the most disturbed psyches."

Following this discovery, the clinician attempted to revive Franz Marc's taste for painting and drawing in the hope of bringing about an improvement in his state. On three occasions he invited him to sit at a table on which he had placed some sheets of paper and some pencils, brushes and paints. Franz Marc sat for two hours without touching any of the objects, his gaze lost in contemplation of the wall facing him. The doctor gave up his experiments.

*

The clinical examination which Franz Marc has undergone at our hands bears witness to a generally satisfying state of health. Cardiological examination shows no anomalies. His blood pressure is normal and pulse regular. The nursing record bears witness to the subject's good constitution and resistance: in all these years he has only caught influenza on one occasion and has never been treated for any other illness.

Having been wounded in 1916 by shrapnel at the battle of Verdun, Franz Marc was trepanned. He has remained deaf in his left ear, and his right ear has suffered a loss of hearing estimated at three quarters of normal. It may be supposed that the latter has worsened mildly with age, even though the examination was unable to show this by reason of the subject's total lack of cooperation, not reacting to any of the questions and requests put by our committee.

We conclude this report by mentioning the fact that Franz Marc has no other relations apart from his wife who comes to visit him on his birthday, 8 February, and on 22 July, which seems to be the date of the anniversary of their first meeting. On questioning, staff report that the subject remains totally indifferent to these visits and does not seem to recognise his wife. For her part, she spends an hour in the subject's company, holding his hand, trying to talk to him, but never receives a response.

Heil Hitler!

Report drawn up by the undersigned
Doctor Emil Löre
and Doctor Ferdinand Breyer,
and sent to the Committee in charge of the
psychiatric asylums of the Reich.

Eglfing-Haar, 7 January 1940

Auction record

The sale of contemporary art organised by Tajan auctioneers on 24 May achieved some exceptional sales, among them a collection of drawings attributed to Franz Marc (1880–1940), one of the leading artists of the German avant-garde of the early twentieth century. A private collector acquired the collection for the sum of 430,000 euros, excluding sales costs, a world record for the artist's drawings.

Article by Fr H.
in *Le Monde*,
28 May 2004

File no. 21-AG-3206
Franz Moritz Wilhelm Marc
Opinion CVT-54-H-45832

The Committee for Hygiene has today, 16 February 1940, examined file no. 21-AG-3206 concerning the patient Franz Moritz Wilhelm Marc, along with the report of Doctors Emil Löre and Ferdinand Breyer drawn up on 7 January 1940 at the time of their visit to the psychiatric institution of Eglfing-Haar within the framework of the public health enquiry into the assessment of patients, and recorded under the class-mark FM-7140-3KTE.

It appears that the committee is not competent to decide in the matter of Franz Marc by reason of the fact recorded in the two enquiry doctors' report recalling the patient's past as a former serving soldier in the Great War.

The committee therefore requests the opinion of

Professor Jennerwein, the sole authorised person in this case to take the correct decision for the good of, and with due respect to, the patient.

Heil Hitler!

For the Committee for Hygiene,
Deputy Director
Doctor Ernst von Haggen

Berlin, 16 February 1940

> "Every biographer has the right to reinvent
> the life that they examine"

On the launch of his new book *Franz Marc: A Biography*
(Carl Hanser, Munich, 2016), *Der Spiegel* met the author
Wilfried F. Schoeller, currently at the centre of a heated
debate instigated simultaneously by historians, the central office of the national archives, and leading figures in
the art market.

Der Spiegel: Do you enjoy scandal?

Wilfried F. Schoeller: Not especially. I like a quiet life, but
I detest lying.

DS: How are you coping with this storm you've found
yourself plunged into?

98

WFS: It will blow over. I've no intention of drowning, I can assure you.

DS: Your book about Franz Marc is presented as a biography, in other words the scrupulous account of a life. Yet you state in your work that the painter did not die in 1940, as all the encyclopaedias tell us, but in 1916. So is it a biography or a novel?

WFS: I'll stick with "biography" – otherwise I would have used the word "novel". But every biographer has the right, the duty even, to reinvent the life that they examine. Before my book, as you have pointed out, it was accepted that Franz Marc had survived being seriously wounded during the war, that he had become asocial in his behaviour and increasingly closed in on himself, to the point of getting himself interned for many years and disappearing in the programme of extermination of lunatics and disabled people initiated by the Third Reich.

DS: But there's evidence of all that.

WFS: Evidence? Let's discuss that, shall we. What evidence? The main body of evidence, which I have been able to examine, is in the federal archives, in the section named *Euthanasie–Verbrechen–Zentralarchiv*[3]. The documents originate from the administrative offices of Aktion T4. In the majority of them – and this has been well known for a considerable time – people's names have been changed, those who signed the reports used pseudonyms constantly, and they distorted the events they narrated, modifying places and dates. The extermination of the sick was an appalling reality that it would be criminal to deny, yet the documents that provide the details, or a record, of that action are more reminiscent of a work of fiction in the way that they borrow from the processes of storytelling. The only evidence that I accept in relation to Franz Marc is that he never again appears, either as an artist or even as a man, after the day in 1916 when he is hit by shrapnel. All the documents that attest to his existence beyond that date are precisely those that have been conserved in those archives and were written by Nazi doctors and their accomplices. I've just told you what I think of them. You won't find any painter who knew him, any art dealer, any critic who can tell you a single anecdote that will provide proof that he did not die at the time I say.

3 "Euthanasia–Crimes–Central Archive".

DS: What interest would the Nazi regime have had in making Franz Marc survive, as it were?

WFS: Firstly, I would ask you to consider that Nazi logic and thought were very different from ours. Reason was not what motivated Nazi actions and decisions. If we accept that, all we can do is put forward hypotheses because, very fortunately, we don't think with the same sick brains that they had. A regime always needs reformed characters, whose admission of repentance rings much more strongly than the words of those who adhere unconditionally and from day one to the new rhetoric. If the regime can suddenly produce an artist who has stopped making the kind of art that is considered "degenerate" and who has chosen, for example, to create no longer, and who even shows enthusiasm when faced with the official art, as one report from Aktion T4 that I reproduce in my book seems to suggest, one can imagine the impact that that might have on people's thinking.

DS: You're referring to the report that mentions a visit by Franz Marc and other patients to the 1937 exhibition of so-called "degenerate" art?

WFS: Absolutely. Pure fantasy.

DS: But why would the Nazis have taken so much trouble to keep Franz Marc in existence, in the most discreet way possible, in an institution, hidden from everyone's gaze? The fact is, it's hardly the best way to make a propaganda tool of him. The world never heard about him. The Nazis made their "Franz Marc" live and die far from any enquiring gaze. It doesn't stack up.

WFS: And what are you and I talking about at this moment, if not that?

DS: We're in 2016. Nazism collapsed more than seventy years ago.

WFS: As collapses go, it's not altogether complete, is it, because we're still debating certain matters, such as this one, relating to what the Nazis did or didn't do. It seems to me that there's an essential thing to understand, which is that those who conceived this regime, and those who served it, had the ambition that it would last for a thousand years. The regime wasn't measured in a human lifespan, and one of its great projects, which we perhaps still haven't fully got the measure of, was to create a memory of humanity which had nothing in common with the actual memory of that humanity. For the regime, it was always about deconstructing what was real as soon as reality failed to serve its purpose and threatened to harm the regime, and substituting instead another reality that obeyed and glorified it.

DS: And to your mind, the "false life" of Franz Marc falls into that category?

WFS: Yes. It, like the innumerable other hoaxes and tricks enacted by the Nazis, is one of thousands of little pebbles, minute grains of sand poured into the mechanism of memory and reality.

DS: But why take so much trouble? Isn't that giving too much importance to the educative impact that Franz Marc's renunciation and his pleasure when faced with examples of official art might have had? Who could it have had an effect on?

WFS: Once again, it's less the impact it has on people than on the general collective memory of humanity. The

Nazis were already reflecting on how history would speak of them. They were working on destroying the present in order to rewrite the future better. There's no doubt that this was the most diabolical part of their enterprise, and we're not through with discovering its consequences: they exterminated millions of human beings, but they also worked towards the extermination of memory.

DS: But the documents that attest to Franz Marc's existence are the same ones that reveal the machinery of extermination the Nazis put in place. Don't you find it paradoxical to forge false documents that also serve to condemn those who fabricated them for deeds that for their part are irrefutable?

WFS: Isn't the best way to authenticate a falsehood, to admit the worst? If the worst is true and one confesses it, then what's less bad is all the more true.

DS: And what do you make of the drawings that were put on sale in Paris in 2004? Experts attributed them with certainty to Franz Marc. They were dated July 1937. That is, twenty-one years after the date of death you're suggesting. You don't even talk about them in your work.

WFS: Because it's not worth it. Because I don't for a second want to give the impression, even by denying their authenticity and existence, that I think they're worth considering. Those drawings don't exist.

DS: You could doubtless be taken to court for those words. A sale took place, the drawings were bought for a fortune, it was all out in the open.

WFS: Out in the open? Did you see the drawings? I didn't. There was no catalogue. They were only put on show for two hours. They were shown behind glass. It was impossible to examine them properly.

DS: An expert authenticated them.

WFS: An expert's opinion, however competent and honest she might be, is not gospel truth.

DS: Are you insinuating that whoever spent more than 400,000 euros was robbed?

WFS: There are plenty of people who are nostalgic for Nazism and who, one way or another, attempt to revive and reintroduce its spirit. Who spent that sum? An anonymous telephone bidder. Who was the seller? He wanted to remain anonymous too. How did he come by the drawings? No-one knows. Have we seen these drawings since? Never.

DS: And so?

WFS: So I'm waiting for someone to prove to me that they exist.

DS: Did you think about the widow of Franz Marc when you were writing your book? She died in 1955. Don't you think she might have reacted violently if she had known your views?

WFS: She's no longer with us.

DS: Yes, I just mentioned that. But imagine for a moment that she were.

WFS: Your question proves that, when it suits you, you're also ready to play fast and loose with the evidence, with the course of people's lives, and with death itself.

DS: But still?

WFS: I have nothing to add.

Interview by Edgar Bahrein
in *Der Spiegel*,
19 April 2016

File no. 21-AG-3206
Franz Moritz Wilhelm Marc
Certificate 231-XTU-GRAQ-56

The secretariat of Professor Jennerwein examined today,
23 February 1940, the file 21-AG-3206 concerning the
patient Franz Moritz Wilhelm Marc along with opinion
CVT-54-H-45832 of the Committee for Hygiene.

It appears from a full examination of all the assembled
documentation and an attentive reading of the medical
reports that it would be of the greatest humanity for
the patient Franz Marc, after a long life which has been
burdened with suffering, to benefit from the programme
put in place to relieve, according to the Führer's will, the
most handicapped and sick patients for whose state
of health there cannot be any hope of remission.

Heil Hitler!

Secretariat of Professor Jennerwein
Berlin, 23 February 1940

Franz Marc (1880–1940),
Bavarian painter and engraver

Franz Moritz Wilhelm Marc was born on 8 February 1880 in Munich. His father, a painter, was noted for working for Ludwig II of Bavaria. He enrolled at the Academy of Fine Arts in Munich but terminated his studies abruptly for unknown reasons.

Fascinated by animals, especially horses, he placed them centre stage in his work. A visit to Paris introduced him to the work of painters Van Gogh and Gauguin, both of whom influenced him.

On his return to Germany he spent time in the company of numerous artists and collectors. In 1910 he moved to Indersdorf, near Dachau. The following year, his meeting with Wassily Kandinsky was a turning point in his career. With Kandinsky he created the artists' group Der Blaue Reiter, and he became known for his variations on the theme of the blue horse. Later, influenced by the work of Italian futurists and the French artist Robert Delaunay, he moved in the direction of abstraction.

At the outbreak of the First World War, he enlisted. Undertaking a reconnaissance mission near Verdun, he was seriously wounded by shrapnel in March 1916.

Having been trepanned and treated at length, he was left completely deaf in his left ear. At the end of the war, despite the exhortations of his gallerist, painter friends and collectors, he decided to abandon his career as a painter, explaining his decision with the words "Neither the world nor men deserve to be painted", which he carved as a woodcut and became his final work, containing these words alone, with no other pattern or figure.

He decided to become a minister, but subsequently abandoned this path. He joined a publicity agency in Berlin as a copywriter, where he worked until early 1920. An incident led him to be confined for the first time in a psychiatric hospital.

From this point onwards, his periods of confinement became more and more frequent, until he was no longer released from the various hospitals to which he was transferred during the rest of his life. He died at Goma-dingen on 16 March 1940 at the age of sixty, apparently from heart failure.

His work, marked by its sense of colour, geometry and movement, enjoyed considerable and widespread success before the First World War before being almost forgotten subsequently. Today we are witnessing a cautious rediscovery of his singular qualities.

Entry by E. K.

in *Encyclopaedia of German Painters and Engravers,*

Vertüge und Schaffler Verlage,

Cologne, 1954

File no. 21-AG-3206
Franz Moritz Wilhelm Marc
Letter copy FMWM-453-A

Director of the Charitable Foundation for Institutional Care,
Doctor Wilfried Schnee
to
Frau Maria Marc, 45 Blumenstrasse, Munich

Dear Madam,

I write to inform you that, in the context of a programme
decided by the highest authorities and intended to place
our residents in locations less exposed to the inherent
risks of war, we have transferred Franz Moritz Wilhelm
Marc, your husband, to an institution where he can
continue to receive the care which is necessary for him.

I am unable, for obvious reasons of security, to

provide you with more precise details concerning his new placement for the moment, but I shall not hesitate to revert to you when it is permissible for me to do so.

Please accept, Madam, the devoted expression of my highest consideration.

Heil Hitler!

Doctor Wilfried Schnee
Berlin, 3 March 1940

"*Reichsleiter* Bouhler and Doctor Brandt are charged with the responsibility of extending the jurisdiction of certain doctors, appointed by name, in order that the patients who, insofar as human understanding can judge in the wake of the fullest diagnosis, are considered incurable, should have the right to a merciful death."

Adolf Hitler, 1 September 1939

Open letter from Doctor Friedrich Untermalher

I am not by nature a person to step out of the discreet obscurity in which I have spent my life, but a recent campaign aimed at casting doubt on the authenticity of drawings by Franz Marc that were offered for sale some years ago, and by association on the honesty of those who organised this sale, compel me to speak publicly.

My name is Friedrich Untermalher and I am seventy-three years old. I was born in Munich and I have never left this city where, for more than forty years, I have practised medicine. It was I who in the early 2000s discovered, on my father's death, in his house, a cardboard folder containing 38 drawings in black crayon, of which a number were embellished with colours. They were all in the same format of forty by thirty centimetres. Eleven of them bore the clearly visible and distinctive signature "Fr Marc".

Not being a specialist in art history, I am nevertheless a lover of painting and of course Franz Marc's name was familiar to me. My father, Viktor Untermalher, was employed from 1933 to 1974 in the psychiatric hospital of Eglfing-Haar as a caretaker. He was a simple and hard-working man who had a great respect for the institution where he was employed, and for the staff and the residents who lived there. Over time, many of them gave him small gifts, most often objects crafted in the workshops to which patients had access. He kept them all in a trunk he stored in his attic, on the lid of which was glued a label with the name, written in his hand, of the psychiatric institution of Eglfing-Haar.

It was in this trunk, among the rag dolls, terracotta tobacco jars and pieces of pine bark scored with a patient's initials that I found the folder with the drawings. My father had never talked about them, any more than he had spoken Franz Marc's name in my hearing or mentioned a famous painter as being one of the residents among whom he spent his days for forty years. My father was an unsophisticated man who was not academic. Doubtless he did not know who Franz Marc was: he must have received the drawings as he received the other residents' gifts, without attaching any more significant value to them, but preserving them all nevertheless over the years, doubtless out of respect for those who had given them to him.

I was not immediately aware of the importance of this discovery. I did not know that after the war Franz Marc had never painted or drawn again. However, as I looked through the contents of the folder I was struck by the drawings' great beauty, their purity, the harmony of the colours where colour was present. Although all the drawings represented animals such as dogs, wolves, foxes, big cats, the scenes radiated none of the violence or cruelty one might have expected from such species; on the contrary they conveyed a harmony and gentleness, as if they had been captured in the dawn of the world, Edenic and peaceful, before mankind placed its death-dealing hand upon it.

It was when I sought the opinion of an art historian of my acquaintance that the latter, at the same time as confirming that the drawings were quite clearly by Franz Marc, informed me that the artist had produced no further work after the end of the First World War and had indeed spent long years at the Eglfing-Haar institute, before dying in 1940, probably as one of the victims of Aktion T4.

On his advice I made contact with Tajan auctioneers, located in Paris, a city which as is well known is one of the important centres of the art market. The auctioneer called in an expert who authenticated the drawings. It was I who expressed the wish that there should be no printed catalogue showing them and who asked that they be exhibited for a limited time only. The drawings had lain hidden away in an attic for decades. The painter, in giving them to my father, had chosen not to make them public. It seemed to me that taking the action I did was continuing to respect his wish.

The sale achieved a high sum that is on the public record. The buyer wished to remain anonymous. He definitely exists, as the cheque for the proceeds of the sale which was sent to me some time later testifies. I have donated the entire sum to three psychiatric institutions in Bavaria. It was in fact the prospect of making these eventual donations that had made me take the decision to sell the drawings. In doing so I intended to pay tribute simultaneously to the artist himself and the years he spent in the world of psychiatry, and also to my father who through his work had tried to remain as close as possible to a suffering humanity.

I will say no more because there is nothing more to say. A recent work, falsely described as a biography, lays out with considerable self-satisfaction, confected beneath its claims to truth, what the author considers to have been the life of Franz Marc. In several interviews that followed the publication of his book, the author has denied the reality of the existence of the drawings and that of their sale.

I hope I have made my own position clear and that I shall never again have to do so in future.

Doctor Friedrich Untermalher

This letter appeared simultaneously
in three European daily newspapers,
Süddeutsche Zeitung, Le Monde
and Corriere della Sera,
in the week of 6 June 2016

File no. 21-AG-3206

Franz Moritz Wilhelm Marc

Letter copy FMWM-541-B

Director of the Charitable Foundation for Institutional Care,

Doctor Wilfried Schnee

to

Frau Maria Marc, 45 Blumenstrasse, Munich

Dear Madam,

I regret to have to inform you of the tragic news of the death of your husband, Franz Moritz Wilhelm Marc, at the Grafeneck institute, Gomadingen, Baden-Württemberg, to which place he was recently transferred.

Franz Marc suffered a cardiac arrest and sadly the doctors were unable to do anything to save him.

He was declared dead on 16 March at 3.12 p.m.

I beg you to accept, Madam, my condolences and those of the foundation of which I have the honour of being the director.

Present conditions not permitting the return of the bodies of those who have died to their families, the decision has been taken that in such cases the body will be cremated, and you will find in the urn accompanying this letter the ashes of your husband.

Please accept, Madam, the devoted expression of my highest regard and this token of my deepest sympathy.

Heil Hitler!

Doctor Wilfried Schnee
Berlin, 3 April 1940

DIE KLEINE

OFTEN WHEN SHE OPENED HER EYES, THE LITTLE girl wondered if it was still the night-time that wasn't over, and the dreams that went with it, or if it was just before morning, and with it the coming of real things. Both states contained lights and sorrows, and she didn't know which was nicer for her, the night-time one or the day-time.

So the still gloomy bedroom, the hollow of the warm bed she was stretching out in, the too-long nightshirt that came down to her feet, the corkscrewed wool socks that covered them and that they flopped around in, and this pillow beside hers, empty but still smelling of the woman, peppery, a bit sharp, with the lingering smell of a fire lit with damp wood – did they all come from a story? A legend like the ones her father used to tell her when she went to see him in the room where he spent a lot of his time, sitting on the floor, on the rugs, with piles of books spread around him, and where he smiled as he caught sight of her and, putting his book down, lifted her onto his knees, stroked her face, kissed her eyelids, called her a new affectionate nickname he'd just made up, and then, in that same room that smelled so nicely of big books, of pipe tobacco and tea, a room lit only by two little bulbs without shades that dangled from the ceiling, rolling their oval eyes, whispered in her ear the fables his own father had told him, in which whole forests started walking to get to a different place, houses talked to each other from street to street, and children flew high in the air in the slipstream of sagacious storks.

Her father's voice always smelled of tobacco. He smoked his pipe while he read, and, being absent-minded and reading from morning till night, he sometimes sat down for the evening meal and started to eat with his pipe still clenched between his teeth, which made her laugh. Her mother laughed too, and the little girl kept her mother's laugh like a piece of bread in a knotted handkerchief, one that holds treasure for those who are famished.

She often imagined the handkerchief and its treasure. It contained her mother's laugh, her father's pipe and smell, the books, her little brother's big eyes, and many other precious things. When she found herself alone and calm, she would knot and unknot the handkerchief's four corners with a solemn expression, put back or take out her treasures, her mother's laugh and her plump breasts that she would often lay her head on to go to sleep, her father's knees as he sat cross-legged like a tailor on rugs whose stiff wool pile she liked to feel under her palm, the stem of the pipe sticking out of his mouth, the books scattered everywhere in the room with the two bulbs, the image of her little brother in his cradle, his plump features hardly visible in the swaddling clothes he was wrapped in.

It wasn't till she ran her hand over her head that she could tell whether she was in her dream or back in reality. In her dream she smelled the curls of her hair, guessed its dark colour, its oily and heavy texture. In the real world, her hand landed on bare, dry skin. Her fingers slid across her bald skull, small like a bird's, with hollows and bumps here and there, bulges and scars as if clumsy hands had darned her, scabs too, which, when she touched them, made her think she was stroking the moon, whose pale and rough roundness she liked in the night-time sky.

Each day she recited to herself her age, which had not yet got to double figures, and her name, along with her mother's name, her father's, and her little brother's first name, the name of the town where she had lived, of the street where the apartment had been, with the cobbler's on the ground floor, and right next door the grocer's, run by the fat man who smelled of garlic and sometimes gave her a sweet, and the shop that sold threads and cloth, and at the far end of the street the synagogue, where her father went every day, with other men.

She said these things to herself, very quickly and several times, so that she didn't lose any of them, so she didn't drop that bit of the treasure in the crack that had opened up in the earth underneath her, between her legs, under her feet, yes, there, where the disappearance had happened. Because nearly everything, people, names, landscapes, words and smells had disappeared, and when she thought about it, bringing back into her head everything she knew and understood about the world, other people and herself, in an effort that made her giddy and sometimes even feverish, she realised that her memory, still in its infancy, was a house without a door or windows and that the wind blew into it from every direction, carrying away with it all that she could not fix solidly to the walls.

Her head had holes. Like her life. In the house of her memory, only crumbled walls remained. Sometimes this made her laugh. Sometimes it made her cry. In the same minute she could go from laughter to tears, or tears to laughter.

She talked in her head. In fact, she only talked there now. Her mouth remained shut all the time, which sometimes made the woman tell her she was like her own father, and the little girl wondered if the woman's father also had a pipe between his teeth, a long warm beard, a wide smile, and hands that were forever deep in books.

She found it hard to imagine the woman with a father because the woman was old. Older than her own mother. Her breasts came down to her stomach and her forehead was criss-crossed by deep lines that ran in all directions, as if someone had wanted to etch her skin with a spike.

Once a week the woman told the little girl to follow her, and the two of them went down the village street and stopped in front of one of the ruins, topped with a sort of big black tooth that had once been a church. Outside was a pile of earth that made a bulge, and on this bulge crosses and flowers had been planted. She and the woman would stand for a moment among the crosses. The woman would clean one in particular. She would wipe a sponge over the wood. Whenever she found a flower in the garden, she would lay it at the foot of the cross. That must have been her father: a cross on some earth.

When the woman slept deeply, she snored, and then the little girl would touch her breasts through the cloth of her nightshirt. They were saggy and soft. Empty of everything. They didn't have any milk. She had checked one night when the woman's nightshirt had ridden up in her sleep and exposed a breast. The little girl had wrapped her lips around the nipple the way her mother, to amuse her, had got her to do when she was breastfeeding her little brother. Then the little girl had felt the warm, slightly sharp-tasting liquid flow into her mouth. But nothing came out of the woman's nipple. Her breasts were old and useless breasts, empty like seed packets you keep even when there's nothing left inside them.

During the day, the little girl played with the hand-kerchief that she kept in her head and that made sure nothing disappeared into the holes in the house of her memory, and that she wasn't swallowed by them either. When the weather was good enough, she would sit on the ground, on a patch of beaten earth next to the barn, under the big iron awning. She would lean back against the brick wall. Facing her, on the left, was the farmhouse from which the woman would appear to go and hang up the washing, throw down some seed or peelings for the hens, set off for the fields or the orchards, or dig in the garden, where plants grew that the little girl didn't know the names of. On the right was the cowshed with the cow, and up against the cowshed was a building that had an even lower roof, which she liked to wander into now and again.

When she was sitting like this, with her back to the barn, when she wasn't cold or hot, and when she had time, she would close her eyes and unknot the hand-kerchief in her head. She would check that none of the contents had got lost: names, faces, moments, the colour of the bedspread on her bed, her little brother's puffed-up face with its swollen eyelids, the sound of her father's voice, and her mother's voice, their smell, the taste in her mouth of the cheese pastries her mother made, and many other things. She reassured herself that everything was still where it should be inside the handkerchief, and that with everything it contained she could relive the life she'd lived, which she did without ever getting tired, combining scenes and names in an order that was different each day, not worrying about whether it was correct or logical.

During these moments she was careful not to run her hands over her head. She put them down flat on the earth, in the dust and bits of straw, because she didn't want to find out, by touching her lovely curly hair or her scabs, if she was in the dream or actually in the real world.

At the woman's house she would use her nails to scratch the candle that was kept in the big drawer of the kitchen table, making lovely smooth ivory-coloured pellets that got soft from the warmth of her round fingers and that she would press into her ears. And the world, as if by a miracle, would suddenly turn its volume down. The woman let her do it, glancing at her from time to time, while she got on with cleaning the oven with a pad of steel wool, or peeled the vegetables, or darned a sock by putting an egg inside it.

Sometimes she also made clothes for the little girl. She would pick a dress out of a trunk in the attic. It smelled of the past. She would make her try it on, pin up the cloth, cut it and re-cut it, then sew up the cuts she had made so that the dress would be the little girl's size, which was tall but thin.

The things the woman did for her were without tenderness or unkindness. She didn't try to be her mother. She didn't try to harm her either. In short, they lived side by side. The woman gave her food, clothes, a bed and a roof. She didn't know what she gave the woman in return, who in any case didn't ask her for anything. Who hardly spoke to her. Didn't kiss her. Didn't stroke her. Didn't hit her. Everything was alright like that.

When the woman wanted to speak to her, she started by waving vigorously in front of her face to attract her attention. This gave her the time to gather everything she had taken out of the handkerchief, put it all back inside the imaginary square of cotton, knot the four corners, and replace the handkerchief in the safest part of her scabby head, in the most secret corner, till the next time, when she would take it out once more to inventory the life she had lost. Then she would remove the balls of wax and return to the real world.

How had she ended up at the woman's? The handkerchief contained nothing to tell her. It might have something to do with some images she had never managed to gather up with the others. A man she doesn't know holds her little brother in his arms and takes her by the hand down a street which isn't her street. A truck that's making a noise like a big insect, in which she dreams, sleeps, wakes up, falls asleep again, squeezed between backs, stomachs, legs, feet. A soldier who gets her off the truck, puts her down on the ground, smiles at her, tells her his name is Viktor, takes her hand and leads her to the edge of a big hole dug in the ground where other people are already waiting. Sudden noises and shouts, then night. Broken sleep in a big bed whose blankets and sheets have been replaced by the bodies of women and men who surround her on all sides, who don't move, who don't smother her, and who give her their warmth for a long time as a cold snow falls from the grey sky, a bed from which she eventually extracts herself, pushing away their arms, their legs, their faces with their eyes closed, being careful not to wake them up. A road along which she is walking, and shivering because she is practically naked, a road she walks down and as she walks all her hair falls out, strand by strand. Finally, a woman's face, somewhere, that bends over her, looks at her, talks to her, but the sounds don't reach her yet. A woman who suddenly straightens up, takes off her coat, covers her in it, and carries her away like a parcel.

And this woman is the woman.

But all that, was it in the dream or in the real world? She never knew whether to slip these pieces into the handkerchief or throw them far away from it.

When the woman went to the village, most often it was to clean the wooden cross on the mound of earth outside the church, stick a flower at its foot and mutter some words. The little girl let the woman do what she needed to do. She raised her head and stared at what was left of the building: a corner of stone wall in which a beam still held up the bells in their molten, mixed-up shapes.

The roof no longer existed. Depending on what kind of day it was, rain or sunlight dripped in the same way over the stone floor, what was left of the pews and the statues, fallen from their plinths and smashed in different-sized pieces, which no-one had got round to picking up. Sometimes the little girl ventured into the nave and lay down full-length on the floor so that her face was at the same level as the decapitated head of a Virgin, made of plaster and painted crudely in pink and gold. Gazing at the face, she lost herself in the smiling eyes of the mother of Christ.

One day, when the woman called her from outside for both of them to go back to the farm, the little girl carried on lying on the floor and the woman had to come into the church to fetch her. She saw her holding the disembodied head tightly to her chest. She tapped her gently on the shoulder because the little girl still had the balls of wax in her ears, but the child did not get up. She kept holding on tightly to the Virgin's head. The woman realised the little girl could stay like that for hours, probably all night too. She fetched the wheelbarrow and made the child understand that she could put the head in it and bring it back to the farm.

The pair of them went home, the woman pushing the wheelbarrow in which the little girl sat cross-legged like a tailor, the plaster head resting between her thighs. She placed it in the bed, not between the woman and her but at the top of the bed on her side. Occasionally during the night, the moonlight crept in between the cracks in the shutter. Then the Virgin's eyes smiled at her and the little girl let her fingers trace her forehead, her nose, her painted mouth. Eventually she fell asleep in mid-caress and in the morning the woman discovered her holding the big cold head with its broken neck tightly to her chest.

When the summer was at its hottest, the little girl disappeared for whole days. The woman didn't try to hold her back. The child had discovered the river and, some way away from the village, a bank of marshes made deeper by black mud, in which tall reeds rose up to the sky.

The water flowed a couple of feet away, slow and ponderous. The child took off her dress, leaving it on the grass, and, completely naked, waded in the mud for hours, never tiring of the sucking noises the sticky substance made. She thrust her hands, her whole arms, her feet and her legs up to her knees into it. To see whole parts of her body disappear like this seemed magical to her.

The mud dried on her skin, forming a black crust. As the hours passed, the carapace cracked, turning her into a creature escaped from the earliest days of the earth. When she smelled herself, the way she had seen dogs do, it smelled strong, of saltiness, earthiness, the ancient silt of the depths. Then the sun turned the mud to dust that her fingers brushed away in the breeze.

She licked her skin, covered with mud. It was salty. It was good. She swallowed her saliva, mixed with the mud. She felt it carry into her body its black grains of heavy clay, rolled by the currents and among which an invisible world of freshwater creatures had died, decayed, decomposed slowly to merge with the rest of matter. She became an animal herself. More immense than her shadow sheltered by the reeds. More frail than the coots and moorhens that scratched the wet earth, leaving the claw-like imprint of their weightless feet.

Occasionally she managed to catch a fish or a frog, trapped in the rhizomes of irises and motuses. She would hold the little creature tight in her hands for a long time, until she couldn't feel it moving anymore. She stared into its eyes to see their flecks of gold, which faded rapidly as it slipped into its deathly sleep. Then she let its body be carried off by the river, which sometimes bore it away on the surface, sometimes gulped it rapidly into its belly. She didn't see any meaning or morality to her action. Didn't feel guilty of anything. She was only in the moment, in the powdery light, in the breeze, the mud, the watercress she munched, turning it into a creamy soup in her mouth. She stayed like this for hours.

When the sun dropped down to the horizon, she returned to the farm, stinking and black, wildly naked, her clean dress in her hand. The woman did not say anything. She took the tub into the courtyard. The little girl got into it. The woman tipped two buckets of warm water over her and gave her the block of soap, the brush, the towel. She ended up falling asleep in the tub, sated with tiredness, with wind and sun and light. Then the woman lifted her out of the water, dried her, picked her up like a laundry basket and put her to bed.

The little girl could feel the woman's gestures, and suddenly the line that separated the dream from the real world became blurred. She kept her eyelids closed. The woman's hands became her mother's hands. A smile formed under her skin but stayed there, never surfacing to appear on her lips or in her eyes. There were, in these moments, deep inside her, things that moved, that were born and died, shapes of thoughts and feelings, a warm confusion sweetened like honey. It all slipped away from her, when she would have liked to cling on to the sensation for ever, and ended up fading in a disappointing fog. She hadn't yet managed to weave a handkerchief fine enough to stop it escaping, nor a sieve to separate the glitter from the dust. Then there came the night, laden with tiredness, and the nothingness that she buried herself in and that still retained, like a distant echo, a taste of mud and summer.

It would have been easy to think the little girl was a ghost who, depending on the day or the time, smelled of soap, pig slurry, mud or apples, alfalfa, fish, shit, milk, squashed raspberries or spring water. She was seen eating worms, caterpillars, butterflies, grasshoppers, gulping down blackbird's eggs with their pale blue shells, in which approximations of featherless nestlings were already waiting, asleep, their eyes glued together.

She lived at the woman's side and the woman lived at her side. They shared the same roof, the same food, the same bed, the same passage of time, the same landscape. War, the crudest of chance's incarnations, had pushed them towards each other.

Sometimes the little girl studied the woman in secret.

She observed her. Afterwards she tried to draw her, without pencils or paints, in her brain. Then she placed this drawing on top of the one of her mother, which she kept deep inside her.

In places the two outlines of their features blurred, in others they diverged, like paths going different ways. Where the faces lay one on top of the other, the little girl noticed that the woman's face weighed heavily on her mother's, erasing it by smothering it. As the weeks passed, her mother's face seemed to dissolve, while her voice stayed intact and clear in the unknotted hand-kerchief, like her father's voice, and his face too because no other man's face had come to crush it.

At times when she became aware of the progressive disappearance of her mother's features, the little girl would run away to the bedroom, curl up in bed and clutch the Virgin's plaster head tightly to her chest. The Virgin always smiled at her with her blue eyes. The little girl put a finger on her lips. But the lips were hard and stayed closed. The kisses she planted there died there immediately.

The handkerchief, folded and tidied away in her brain, held many things but they were things that no longer moved, the way that clothes that have lost the bodies that used to inhabit them still keep a trace of their shape and their smells, but not much. Everything the little girl kept in the handkerchief reminded her of what had happened before, and over there. But over there was gone. There was only here.

In about the middle of August she stopped going to the river. But she still left in the morning and came back in the evening, late, her skin no longer covered in a flaking crust but in pale yellow dust, the dust of the dry earth of the stubble fields, of the ash-blond straw that likes to gather in the skin's creases in the elbow, and the neck and groin, between the thighs, around the sides of the nose. She didn't stink this time. She smelled of the air and the country paths, of the thickets, the storms, peppery sweat. She looked like a female faun. The sun had browned her shaved head and her scarred face had begun to look like over-baked bread. Her eyes, in the middle of all this, looked even blacker.

All her walks had a single purpose in mind, to draw this place inside her, to put things where they belonged: trees, fields, forests, farms, beds of streams, ponds, springs, marshes, vegetable patches, bridges, mills. To forget the handkerchief and to draw a map which would make it pointless.

When she had discovered the factory building, a long way from the village and at the very limit of the ground she could cover in a single day, she had walked around it for a long time before daring to go in. What stopped her was the noise of what sounded like a monster that was coming from the building, which was surrounded by two rows of high wire fencing that had been knocked down and cut in the middle. It was deserted. The main door was open, and a wailing sound, halfway between a plea and an exhausted roar of fury, was coming from it at the same time as a thin crackling smoke that smelled of metal, motor oil and burnt elastic.

She went inside and was struck by the beauty of the shapes arranged across the floor in perfect alignment. They were made of glass crowns, piled one on top of another, and replicated themselves the length of the building, linked to each other by a sort of cord braided in a black substance. Some were still smoking a little and sizzling, from time to time spitting a ball of light that fell to the ground in a shower of blue embers. As they flew up and died away, these sharp cracks and sparks covered the continuous rumble, with its deep bass, being emitted by the cube of concrete in which all the cords that joined the glass installations converged.

Next to one of the glass crowns lay a black shape that the little girl stared at for a long time before making out, bit by bit, in what she had thought was a big piece of burnt wood, the body of a man.

She wasn't afraid of what she had discovered, because the corpse did not resemble a human being very much anymore, with its head half its original size and the extremities of its limbs balled into charred stumps, its feet and hands missing. The man was slightly hunched over. What still existed of his left arm was held out towards the crown of glass, and between this crown and the body was a big iron bar, which seemed to indicate that the man had attempted to do something, and the little girl, despite her young age, understood that a link must exist between the man's death, the iron bar, the crown of glass and the black cords sputtering with irregular showers of lights.

The carbonised corpse came to signify for her, in the landscape she had been making it her task to survey for several days, the outer limit of this world, and the factory a sort of frontier post inhabited by a dead customs officer who had attempted the impossible and whose mere presence was enough to discourage any potential traveller from going any further, in one direction or the other. She came back every day to visit him and carried on visiting him till the cold rains of autumn began. She went into the building, sat next to him, and scrutinised every centimetre of his black shape, as if she wanted to print an exact drawing of him inside herself. Occasionally some spitting sparks reached her, but she felt no burning sensation, hardly even a prickling that stopped as soon as the electric fireflies went out.

Sitting in the company of this puzzling corpse she realised that she had forgotten the handkerchief, and what was inside it, the traces of her loved ones, and the sorrows linked to the presence of those traces, to their safekeeping and their dwindling.

In the evening, once she had come back and the woman was giving her some soup after having washed her, the man's dry, blackened body sat between the two of them. The little girl got a dish from the dresser, put it next to hers and poured a little bit of soup into it for the dead man. The woman didn't interfere and asked no questions. The little girl talked to the corpse. She told it about the woman, the cow, the frogs and the mud, the taste of grasshoppers, the Virgin and how her eyes were never closed, and plenty of other things which weren't in the handkerchief, which didn't need to be there because she'd lived those things or discovered them since she had arrived in the country of here, with her father and mother no longer with her.

The dead man, who didn't look like a man, could not hear what she wanted to say to him. And because you could not make out his ears anymore from the rest of his burnt skull, which looked very much like a big lump of charcoal, the little girl didn't even have to say the words out loud. It wouldn't have been any use. She said them in her head, to herself.

It was enough for her.

She was certain that that way the man could take them in and hear them, and use them to carry on living through her in his death.

TO THE READER

The texts collected here were written between 2016 and 2020.

"Gnadentod" ("Mercy Killing") is a counterfactual story that appeared in a collection entitled L'avant-garde perdue (The Lost Avant-garde), originated by Nicolas Ehler, director of the Goethe Institute at Nancy.

It is of course a work of fiction. Nevertheless, though the story is invented, everything about Aktion T4 and its execution procedures is true. Hitler's letter dated 1 September 1939 is real, and was the order that launched the operation to exterminate psychiatric patients.

The term "Gnadentod" that provides the text's title is the same one Hitler used. The reports and letters of the various doctors implicated in the process of evaluation and decision-making are fictional but closely resemble existing documents.

I have also taken the liberty of using the name Wilfried F. Schoeller, who really did write on Franz Marc.[4] I have attributed to him words, standpoints and actions which are evidently not his own. I ask his forgiveness for having done so without asking his permission. I hope he will discern no malice in the use I make of him as a character, but on the contrary a tribute to his work and scholarship.

The Tajan auction house, and the newspapers and magazines whose names I have used, never played the roles that I give them, nor published the articles and interviews I invented.

"Sex und Linden" ("Sex and Limes") was commissioned by the Joseph Haydn Foundation of Basel for the project "Haydn 2032" which each year stages a series of concerts and recordings of the composer's works, around which a writer is invited to imagine a story.

★

4 Wilfried F. Schoeller, *Franz Marc*, Carl Hanser, Munich 2016.

"Ein Mann" ("A Man"), "Irma Grese", and "Die Kleine" ("The Little Girl") are previously unpublished.

Although the times and the conditions under which each of these texts was written were different, they turn on themes and ideas that have been important to me for a long time: first and foremost that of the incoherence of history and the roles men play in it, or rather think they play in it. Also the idea of "the people", the nation or human group, an idea about which I feel considerable scepticism, preferring to see each individual as a grain of sand in the midst of a big pile – compact or friable, depending on the moment – who one random shove can put in a position they could have never imagined. The idea of guilt too, which is not to be understood in this context in its moral sense any more than it is to be envisaged as contemporaneous with the action it relates to: it's more to be read as the result of a decanting that the present carries out in relation to the past, and upon which history bases its principles and its orthodoxy. Finally the idea of memory – consubstantial with the activities of writing and reading, whether it's about individual memory, whose functioning for me constitutes one of the greatest human mysteries, or collective memory, which sometimes weighs with unbearable force on the life of the group that has constructed it and lives with it, and then again can seem emptied of its painful and awkward stuff, to the point of being simultaneously like a screen of fog and a comfortable drug.

When I collected these texts and laid them out in front of me, the way you lay out playing cards, I was struck by the echoes that connected them. So I reworked them, more substantially in some cases, less in others, to reinforce these links between them. Having done that, it struck me that they formed a genuine book, a sort of novel which I deliberately left incomplete, and at the heart of which is a call to the reader to fill the gaps by becoming a writer themselves. All of them tell us about fragments of existence in a century and a geography that are unique, and we discover little by little that these fragments resonate with each other, in a distant way, deeply or shallowly, under the headings of chance or coincidence. All of them create spaces of uncertainty. The character of Viktor becomes the symbol of this: in the course of the stories certain elements encourage us to believe this is the same person, others show us the opposite. So what sort of truth about him does that leave us with? And beyond him, about all truth? It seemed to me to be a metaphor for our lives, which we think we know but which we control so badly and which can, depending on the angle at which we shine a light on them, reflect back at us in a multiplicity of ways.

Germany in the twentieth century is the context for this book for two reasons. One, because in no other place have the themes I have talked about found their tragic embodiment with the intensity they found there. And two, because having been myself a neighbour of that country since my childhood, I have developed a relationship both of attraction and dread towards its landscapes, its culture, its language and its history, unlike any relationship I have with any other country in the world. Germany for me has always been a mirror in which I see myself not as I am, but as I could have been. In that sense, it has taught me a great deal about myself.

I will end by saying that the term "fantasia" in the book's title is to be understood in its musical and poetic sense, which describes, as is generally known, a work in which the author's subjectivity dominates and which liberates itself from adhering to strict rules of composition or harmony.

Philippe Claudel
March 2020

PHILIPPE CLAUDEL is a university lecturer, novelist, film director and scriptwriter. He has written fourteen novels that have been translated into several languages. In 2009 his film "I've Loved You So Long", which draws upon Claudel's eleven years teaching in prisons, won the BAFTA Award for Best Film Not in the English Language. Among his novels, *Grey Souls* won the Prix Renaudot in France, the American Gumshoe Award and the Swedish Martin Beck Award. *Brodeck's Report* won the *Independent Foreign Fiction Award* in 2010.

JULIAN EVANS is a translator, biographer and travel writer. His book *Transit of Venus* has been described as "the best modern travelogue about the Pacific". He translates from French and German, including Michel Déon, André Gide and Norbert Gstrein. He is a recipient of the Académie Française Prize for the Advancement of French Literature and is a Royal Literary Fund Consultant Fellow.